THE
ARTIFICIAL
MAN

L. P. Davies

SBS SCHOLASTIC BOOK SERVICES
New York Toronto London Auckland Sydney

Copyright © 1965 by L. P. Davies. This edition is published by Scholastic Book Services, a division of Scholastic Magazines, Inc., by arrangement with Doubleday & Company, Inc.

1st printing September 1968

Printed in the U.S.A.

1

IT WAS AN AWAKENING to a morning like any other, a returning to the contented awareness of familiar surroundings, to the security of a room filled with somnolent sunshine, to the small remote sounds of the house coming to life. His hands clasped at the back of his neck, Alan lay and watched the slow play of shadow-branches on the sun-gilded ceiling. It was a good thing to do, spend the first minutes of waking in bringing the past up to date and planning the new day ahead. A kind of mental stock-taking, a gathering of thoughts and impressions.

And the background of the coming day would be the background of all those that had gone. Only the details, the trivialities, would differ. He would wash, shave, and dress, and go down to the kitchen where Mrs. Low, his housekeeper, would be mildly impatient to have breakfast out of the way so that she could start on the comfortable routine of housework. That was how the day would open, how yesterday had started, and the one before that. For as far back as memory was prepared to take him without conscious effort.

Sliding out of bed he padded to the open window to rest his elbows on the sill. No mist this morning, the outlines of the enfolding hills sharp and clear. A hint of rain, perhaps . . . Lee would be pleased. Lee who lived next door and spent time spared from his studio in pottering about his garden. Who was down there now, beyond the low privet hedge, on hands and knees on the gravel path that bisected his lawn, oil can poised over decrepit mowing-machine.

"High time you treated yourself to a new one," Alan called down, and the other glanced up, coal-black hair as unruly as ever.

"We can't all be prosperous scribblers," Lee Craig retorted pleasantly, smiling his peculiar sideways smile. "There are those of us who have to watch our budgets. Finance, at the moment, is a sore point in the Craig *ménage*. Sybil speaks of a new hat. I am in some need of a new suit." He came to his feet, stretching, one hand clamped to the small of his back. "The outcome is a foregone conclusion. I shall have to make my rags last a little while longer." He touched the machine with a sandaled foot. "And old faithful here will have to weather at least another summer."

"No mist this morning," Alan observed, his eyes back on the hills. "Could be a sign of rain."

"Wouldn't do any harm." Lee turned back from a brief inspection of the horizon to peer upward again, shading his eyes with the back of his hand. "You look like you've only just tumbled out of bed. Respectable citizens have got through an hour's work by now."

Alan grinned cheerfully. "I don't notice your working yourself to death."

"You will." The other thrust the oil can into the hip pocket of his stained flannels and grasped the handles of the machine to cut a token vicious swath through the grass.

"You'd think," he commented aggrievedly, stopping and leaning back, "that the bright boys would come up with some kind of grass that grows an inch and then stops. I'll have a cup of coffee with you when you've pulled yourself together."

Nodding, Alan withdrew from the window. That was how almost every day started, with a brief exchange of pleasantry with his next-door neighbor. And that was Lee Craig, freelance commercial artist — yet unimaginative enough to call his house "Mon Repos" — fortyish, tall, with ungainly limbs that gave the impression of being wire-attached to his lanky body; with a narrow face composed of brown flesh laid thinly on angular bones, a smile that was all his own and an almost always uncombed mass of black hair.

Stripped to the waist, running water into the bathroom washbowl, Alan thought how pleasant it was to have a man like Lee for a friend. And Lee's wife — Sybil . . . He reached to turn off the tap. For a moment her image refused to take shape. Then the picture fell into place; over-bright dresses, short dark hair tinged at the sides with grey;

a kind of brittle, porcelain beauty. A background wife. . .

Drying his face with the rough towel brought a tingling sensation to one side of his forehead. He looked sideways in the mirror. The thin line of the scar was white against the faint flush of surrounding flesh. He turned his head to inspect the matching scar at the other side. That was not nearly so pronounced.

The face that stared back at him was suddenly that of a stranger. He postured, seeking some point of recognition. This was the Alan Fraser that the world saw. A solid nose; a full mouth; eyes as anonymous as the face, and a face that was like any other. Smooth complexioned — despite its thirty-six years — and now that the towel-flush was fading, oddly colorless. Only the hair to lift it from the rut of mediocrity; thick, luxuriant, stiff, and reddish-brown. Familiar features that refused to coalesce into a familiar whole. Frowning a little, Alan opened the cabinet to take out his electric razor.

Afterward, coming out of the bathroom, he misjudged the sweep of the door, slamming it with unnecessary violence. As he crossed the landing Mrs. Low's voice came from below. "You nearly ready, Mr. Fraser?"

"Two minutes," he called back, and then, in the bedroom, opening the wardrobe and selecting clothes, he wondered if other people ever experienced those odd, disconcerting moments when their own faces suddenly took on the obscurity of strangeness. He supposed that it must be a normal thing.

In the kitchen, Lee, lounging, cup in hand, against the open back door, nodded without speaking. Mrs. Low, solidly curved beneath white apron and pink blouse, brought a laden plate from the top of the stove, setting it on the table and fussily adjusting knife and fork.

"The bacon's crisped," she apologized. "I'm sorry about that. I know you prefer it soft. I thought I heard you up earlier."

"He was hanging out of the window." Lee put in. "In a state of flagrant dishabille. If that's the right expression. Words aren't my strong point. How's the book coming, old son?"

There was a letter by Alan's plate. It had to be from his agent — there was no one else to write to him.

"I've roughed out the first chapters," he replied absently, sliding a knife under the flap.

"If you gentlemen will excuse me," Mrs. Low said from the passage door, "I'll see about making a start on my bedrooms."

Alan propped the letter against the milk jug. Kitch had written to say he had placed a short story with *Tomorrow* for forty guineas. Alan frowned slightly at the amount. It was less than he had expected, but it should be enough to keep the wolf from the door for another couple of weeks. Kitch also mentioned that he was waiting anxiously for the first chapters of the novel. Alan slipped the letter into his pocket.

"So we're still in the roughing-out stages," Lee remarked conversationally. "How long before we get down to it in earnest?"

"Early days yet." The bacon was more than crisped, the lean was hard and brittle. "I want to get the feel of it before I start writing."

"I know what you mean. I'm the same with my stuff. First a rough outline in my head, then the first tentative touches of pencil to paper, with my instinct being my guide. What's the book to be about?"

Alan had to think about that. At odd moments, over the past few weeks, he had typed background notes. Right now the thing was only a miscellany of ideas. But one thing was clear enough . . .

"It's a fictional biography," he said.

The other pursed judicious lips. "Doesn't sound your line of country, Alan. I mean, you seem to be on a good thing with your science-fiction stuff, so why risk changing?" He moved from the door to deposit his empty cup in the sink. "But being a fair-minded person I'm prepared to admit you might be able to pull it off." He turned, cocking an eyebrow at a sudden thought. "You could combine the two. If you see what I mean. The biography of a Martian. Have you thought up a title for it yet?"

"I don't write about Martians, not even for the pulps." Alan shook his head. "And no — I haven't got the title yet. No names at all yet, not even for the chief character."

The sunlit rectangle of the door darkened.

"There was a rumor," Sybil broke in after her silent approach, "that someone was thinking about mowing my lawn." She folded bare brown arms across her over-tight, bright blue dress and regarded her husband with an accusing eye. "I thought I'd find you here." Turning to Alan she exchanged mock severity for a bright smile. "And how are you this morning, Alan?"

"Fine." He nodded to the stove. "Coffee?"

"You're confusing me with someone else," she told him. "I'm not the champion coffee drinker of Bewdey."

"I am not frittering my time away as your tone suggests," Lee said with dignity. "I was discussing his new book with Alan and favoring him with the benefit of my advice. We have decided that it is to be a fictional biography set fifty years in the future."

Alan pushed his plate aside. "Why fifty years ahead?"

Lee ignored the interruption. "As yet we haven't decided upon a title. We are waiting until we have found a name for our main character. We shall then use that name as the title. A strong name is called for. . . . Forceful — suggestive of broad shoulders and jutting jaws."

Alan came to his feet.

"The rough notes are on my desk," he said dispassionately. "Why don't you just rip them up and write the blasted thing yourself?"

He and Lee understood each other. That's how it had always been.

"For two pins," Lee mused thoughtfully, "I'd do just that."

Sybil stepped back into sunlight. "Out!" She pointed sternly "Lawn!"

Lee became a man cowed into submission, meekly allowing himself to be led away.

Alan went into the passage, and in the hall came upon an odd moment of indecision. The right-hand door, or the left? The thing fell into place. In the study, going toward his desk, he fought a small wave of dizziness. Mrs. Low appeared from nowhere, a glass of water in one hand, two white tablets on the palm of the other. Alan took them automatically, placing them on his tongue and then sipping the water. He lowered himself to the round-backed chair. The dizziness had passed. A humming outside was the vacuum cleaner and Mrs. Low back at work again.

The sheaf of notes lay on the desk between calendar and typewriter. Changing the leather-backed perpetual calendar was the first job. Sliding the magnetic rectangle reminded him of an earlier decision. It would be a good idea to keep a diary of the progress of the novel. From one of the drawers, after some fumbling, he took out a small notebook, opening it and heading the first page: Monday, June 13, 1966. He wrote slowly, holding the slim pen clumsily.

Replacing the diary he picked up the notes. Reading them he fished in his pocket for cigarettes, lighting one and then coughing as the warm smoke hit the back of his throat. This was the first time he had read the roughed-out background as a whole. He found the lack of continuity disappointing — little enough on which to start writing the novel. The random notes refused to become a coherent whole. Some were so obscure that he could barely recall writing them. He ran a ruthless pen through the over-verbose description of a nameless village church. The cigarette forgotten he went through the sheets, deleting violently, and coming to the last page, turned back to reread what was left.

A child born in a wooden shack in a nameless village. Not a thatched-cottage village like Bewdey, but a handful of decrepit wooden shacks and a lonely railway that arrowed across a desert to a distant horizon. "Australia," he inserted in the margin, and added a question mark.

Alan stubbed out his cigarette and leaned back, trying to picture the child. He found it oddly impossible. He was also aware of a lack of confidence in his own ability to tackle a novel.

But Kitch thought he could do it, and so, apparently, did Lee. And Lee was always right. His notion of combining biography with science fiction was a good one. It wouldn't be the first time Lee had proffered assistance disguised as a challenge. His idea of a fifty-year-ahead background was a challenge.

What would the world be like in half a

century's time? Would the next fifty years change life as much as the fifty years past had done? Alan painted pictures on his mind. All things considered, mankind had taken only a short step forward during the past fifty years. The next fifty should see nothing too revolutionary. And Lee, with his knowledge of design, would be able to help by projecting that knowledge into the future.

Alan went into the hall. Chamois in hand Mrs. Low turned from polishing a mirror, smiling, asking: "Stuck again, Mr. Fraser?"

He fought down mild resentment at this stock question of hers, knowing that it was only her way of trying to show sympathy and understanding. He knew her as well as he knew himself. Apart from the few months spent in hospital there had never been a time when Mrs. Low hadn't been as much a part of his existence as the clothes he wore, the house in which he lived, even the very air he breathed. In turn, she had been midwife, nursemaid, even nurse for a time, and now housekeeper.

And so he smiled back at her. "For once in my life I'm not stuck, Mrs. Low. I think I may be on to something good. But it'll take a deal of thought."

She looked at the gilt sunburst clock. "If you're thinking of going for a walk then, don't be too long. I'll be making a drink for you as usual at eleven."

"I'll be back before then," he promised and, opening the door, stepped out into the sunlight.

Lee had finished mowing his lawn. The air was filled with the warm richness of newly cut grass. Alan walked down the graveled drive to rest his arms on the gate. The lane, tree-lined, curving out of sight on either hand, was empty. Before setting out on the small adventure of a stroll there was time for the pleasure of another stocktaking.

This was Bewdey, the handful of cottages that was little more than a hamlet, where he had been born and lived all his life. The hills, the trees, the spreading fields, and the few dwellings were as familiar to him as the lines on his hand. To the right, hidden by the bend, the tiny post office with Peter Clamp — always his name in full — waiting for customers behind his grille and sweet-bottle counter. And beyond — nothing but the lane, winding its way between encroaching foothills to link with the main road that led to Cradhill.

And to the left. . . . George Tarvin's General Stores and the police cottage where Constable Cowen lived alone. The Cot — the Major lived there, also alone — and Clove Cottage which had stood empty for some years now, and Rose Cottage, once let each summer to strangers, now occupied permanently by Tony Verity, an artist. And beyond the little community the lane narrowed, becoming grass-tufted from disuse, narrowing, finishing at the dead end of the rusty-padlocked gates of Old Oak Farm, that had stood empty, gradually falling into neglect, for ten years or more.

And that was Bewdey — that was the story of his life. There was a world beyond the bramble barriers of the hills, but it was of no importance. He had been born here; he was content to live and die here.

Opening the gate, Alan paused, for now there was a choice to be considered. To the right, and a walk past the post office? Or the other way, with the possibility of a chat with the Major, or Tony Verity, or with George Tarvin in the doorway of his shop? He turned to the left, walking slowly in the direction of the cottages and the derelict farm, drawing in the morning freshness, savoring each moment as if each were a new experience.

At the sound of a vehicle coming up behind he stepped into the grassy verge without bothering to glance back, knowing it could only be the daily delivery van from Cradhill on its way to Tarvin's stores. The rickety once-green van, with faded, scrolled letters on its side, "Liffy & Brand. Wholesale Grocers," slowed as it came abreast, Fred leaning out, grinning hugely, calling: "Out for your constitutional, Mr. Fraser?"

Alan stepped back into the road, quickening his pace to keep level, prepared to enjoy the usual few moments of lighthearted badinage with the plump-faced, ever-smiling Fred Tolley.

"Making the most of what little spare time I have," he replied.

"Your life's all spare time," Fred retorted

cheerfully. "How's the scribbling coming along these days?"

"Still managing to make both ends meet."

"Didn't you say once you were thinking of having a bash at a novel?"

"At this very moment," Alan told him gravely, "I am in the throes of its birth pangs."

"You sound as if you could use the services of a midwife," the other called back over his shoulder as the van accelerated away. Alan raised his hand as it disappeared round the bend in a little swirl of dust.

By the time he reached the bend, it was out of sight. The next curve in the lane brought the cottages into view, with Major Holt's the first on the right, and the Major himself, hidden at first by the hedge, straightening from the rockery that filled his tiny front garden to remove his spectacles with a flourish before mopping a huge, over-florid and perspiring forehead with a handkerchief taken from the breast pocket of a thick tweed jacket.

"Hot," Major Holt commented briefly. "Damned hot. Eh?" Returning the handkerchief he set large hands on his hips and glared down at the rockery. "Damned weeds. Fast as you root 'em out, damned seed comes blowing in from the fields."

Alan peered over the hedge. "You manage to keep it looking nice," he said generously. "What's that blue flower?"

"Which?" The other followed his eyes. "That. Gentian, I think. Damned stupid

Latin name when I bought it." He replaced his spectacles. "No time for that sort of thing. How's the writing?"

Alan matched brevity with brevity. "So-so."

"Hell of a way to make a living," observed the Major pleasantly but unsmilingly. His parade-ground features rarely relaxed their military stiffness. "Not my cup of tea." He shook his head, the sunlight glinting on sparse silver hair. "Something more substantial. Eh? Security of income. Pensions." He inspected his watch. "Time for my morning drink. Care to join me?"

Alan explained that Mrs. Low would have a drink waiting for him on his return, thanked the Major for his offer and resumed his walk. There was no visible sign of Tony Verity, but from the open front window of the parlor that had been converted into a studio came the sound of his voice raised in raucous, tuneless song. A little farther on, Tarvin was busy sweeping his cobbled forecourt. A nostalgic spicy smell came from the open door behind.

Tarvin leaned on his broom. "Grand morning, Mr. Fraser." The breeze, what little there was, moved the soft black frizz of his hair. He had a broad, flat nose and a country-swarthy face that creased into a mask of lines when he smiled.

"The Major" — Alan nodded backward — "seems to find it too warm for comfort."

"An overloaded waistline," Tarvin grinned. "Too much sweet stuff. Which reminds me.

You might let Mrs. Low know her biscuits have just come in. She'll know the ones."

"I'll do that," Alan promised.

Another five minutes took him to the end of the lane, to where ragged briar hedges did their best to meet, where grass grew between rubble and the drunken but still sturdy gates barred further progress. Ahead, across a wilderness of grass and scrub, the deserted farm buildings were an eyesore against the background of trees. Behind, the hills rose steeply, fold upon fold of purple and gold and brown. With the gate to lean against, a rise in the ground affording a view of most of the valley, it was pleasant to rest here awhile, the sun warm on his shoulders, and think about nothing in particular. It was something he had done a million times.

But this time it was different. A chain of thought started with Tarvin's message for Mrs. Low, drifted to Mrs. Low herself, and that was comfortable and pleasant, but then returned to Tarvin, and the biscuits that had presumably just been delivered. And that brought in Fred and his little green van, and that was uncomfortable and almost frightening, because something was very wrong.

The van had passed him on its way to Tarvin's shop, and there were no side roads and no way out here at the top, and the van — he was quite positive about this — hadn't passed him on its way back. It hadn't left the valley, and it had been nowhere in sight. The lane had been completely empty.

The van had disappeared.

2

Lee laughed at first, loudly, obviously seeing the thing as an amusing puzzle and not as something to become upset about. Alan's worried face caused him to turn off the laughter, but he still retained his sideways smile.

"The writer's imagination," he said. "Looking for mysteries where none exist. Mountains out of molehills —"

And then he became completely serious, which was an unusual thing for him.

"All right, old son," he said gently. "So let's see if we can sort it out for your peace of mind. Fred's van comes up behind you as you are going up the lane —"

"I had a few words with him," Alan inserted.

"It passes you, and you carry on, right up to the farm —"

"I stopped to talk to Major Holt. And to Mr. Tarvin."

"And there's the answer to your mystery," Lee stated with an air of certainty. "Fred came back while you were chatting with the galloping Major. Or while you were with our tame grocer."

Alan shook his head. "No."

They were on Lee's front lawn. Sybil, arms folded, stood by the rustic arch, listening intently.

"It could easily have passed without your noticing it," she offered. "Familiarity — you know. Unless . . ." She paused significantly.

"I'd thought about that," Alan said in a small voice. "I didn't have one of my blackouts. I'm sure of that."

Lee looked uncomfortable. Sybil, muttering something about having to see about lunch, turned and went into the house.

"How long since you had the last one?" Lee asked quietly.

"Quite a while ago." Alan put his hand on his forehead. "I can't remember when. I did have a dizzy spell this morning, but it went almost immediately.

"You do seem to have been better lately." The other nodded slowly. "We don't want anything to upset the even tenor of our ways." He clicked his fingers as a thought struck him. "There's one way we can solve the mystery —"

"How?"

"Come with me," Lee said briskly, and led the way across his lawn. In the hall he picked up the telephone.

"Peter Clamp? Craig here. Look, will you put me through to the firm of grocers that Fred Tolley works for? I forget their name. . . . That's the one. . . . No, I don't know the number. Look it up." He winked broadly at Alan. "What do you think the post office pays you for?"

He leaned against the wall while he waited, whistling a few bars of tuneless melody. Then:

"Hello? My name is Craig; I'm speaking from Bewdey. Could I have a word with Mr. Tolley?"

"They're getting him," he informed Alan. "So he's got back all right." He turned back to the phone. "Fred? Lee Craig here. Look, we have a little mystery on our hands —"

Alan went to the front door to stand looking out at the empty lane. There had been no blackout. He had had enough experience of them to know that. There was a time and a place when you were doing something, and then another time and sometimes another place when you were doing something else. And in between there was nothing. Only the after-knowledge of an unaccountable gap. But always there was that after-knowledge of a small missing part of your life. But this morning he could account for every second. There had been no gap. He became aware of Lee at his side.

"According to Fred you were talking to the Major when he came back," Lee said evenly. He rested his hand lightly, reassuringly on Alan's shoulder. "If I were you I'd mention it to Dr. Crowther when he shows up this afternoon. Just to be on the safe side. You know?"

Alan moved his shoulders in an indefinite

gesture. There was no point in trying to argue. His forehead felt tight and he pressed his fingers to the mounds of his brows, feeling the pulse hard beneath.

"Try not to worry," Lee said solicitously. "Crowther knows the form — he'll sort it out. If you like, I'll have a word with him first. At least it'll save you going through it all again for his benefit."

The doctor arrived about the middle of the afternoon. Hearing the sound of the car stopping outside, Alan slipped from the bed where he had been resting since lunch to go over to the window. Crowther, hatless as usual, over-solid, with balding head, massive forehead, and oddly waxen features, was easing himself out of the small black sedan before turning to collect his case from the rear seat. And Lee was waiting to talk to him. The two came slowly up the drive, the doctor with his face puckered worriedly.

And in the living room, some ten minutes later, with the usual examination over:

"Craig mentioned this morning's incident," Dr. Crowther said smoothly, replacing the stethoscope in his bag.

Alan continued buttoning his shirt without replying.

The other closed his case with a click. "I know I've asked you this before, but do you dream very often?"

Alan shook his head. "Hardly ever."

"And what about your memory? Can you

recall the accident in any detail — perhaps see the other car coming toward you — see the flames?"

He broke off. "I'm sorry. I had to see your reaction." He lowered his bulk into a chair. "Anything I do or say is only for your own good. I brought you into the world, and I've taken care of you ever since. But I have to know just how vivid your memories are."

"Ten years is a long time," Alan said steadily.

"You're trying to say the memory is fading. A good thing in one way, bad in another. Your conscious mind has taught itself to forget. But your subconscious is a very different matter." He leaned forward impressively. "From time to time it tries to remind you. But your conscious mind rejects it. It applies anaesthesia and so you have a blackout.

"I know that we have gone over all this a hundred times before. But now it would seem we have reached a new stage. Blackouts vary in duration. Up until now yours have varied between half an hour and two days. The indications now are that they are becoming of shorter duration with increasingly long intervals between. A good sign. This morning you experienced one that lasted only a few seconds."

He leaned back, ponderously satisfied with his diagnosis. "That should have put your mind at ease. All right?"

"All right," Alan agreed woodenly.

"Try not to worry." The doctor came laboriously to his feet and picked up his case. "I'll leave a fresh supply of tablets with Mrs. Low. I'll drop in again tomorrow." His smile was a condescending creasing of flabby cheeks. "I don't think you realize just how much interest I take in your case. I make a special journey out here to the wilds just to see you. So it's up to you to follow my instructions."

When he had gone, Alan went to the study and sat at his desk. But he was unable to work. Something was troubling him, some vague worry that intruded on his thoughts. Nothing to do with the van, for he had to accept the doctor's explanation for that. Something different. Something that wasn't as it should be. . . .

Lee came in breezily, wanting to know what Crowther had had to say for himself. Alan explained briefly.

"So that's all right," Lee bent over his shoulder. "Back to the novel then?"

"That's it." Alan offered his cigarettes. "I wanted to ask your help."

Lee flicked his lighter. "I'm flattered. Ask away."

"What will things be like in fifty years' time?"

"That's a stiff one." Lee hooked a chair with his foot, dragged it toward him and sat down. "I don't know, though. Merely a question of sorting out present-day problems and then projecting them into the future. And our biggest potential problem —"

"Population explosion?"

"I had the cold war in mind. But you could be right. We're thinking about the year —" He closed his eyes.

"2016," Alan supplied.

"2016. Has quite a ring about it. So what will we have then? Overpopulation, with the provision of food being an even greater problem than living space. Which obviously means some permanent forms of rationing. Rationing means identity cards and masses of documents. Everyone will have a number which they'll probably use more than their own names. John Henry number. All right so far?"

"A kind of super Welfare State." Alan grimaced distaste. "It's logical though. Keep going."

"Right. So what else will we have? Birth control for the masses. Inevitable. Which means rigid State control. Even a kind of Police State. How does that sound?"

"Let's talk about the cold war," Alan said. "Will Russia still be sitting on the fence?"

"With China the real villain of the piece. Only by then she will have spread out at the expense of adjacent countries, maybe even India. China in Asia. Sinoasia. How does that sound? Have you found a name for your chief character yet?"

"Not yet. First things first."

"I'd have thought that would have been the first. Have it your own way. The Sino-asian Peoples Republic then. Sinoa for short."

"Tucked away behind a Bamboo Curtain,"

Alan supplied, and Mrs. Low came in with the afternoon tablets.

"Cheers," Lee said as Alan drank the water. "Mrs. Low, what do you think people will be wearing fifty years hence — what kind of clothes?"

"Clothes?" She paused by the door. "In fifty years' time? I've never given it a thought, Mr. Craig. They'll get to be flashy, I suppose. Bright colors and very shiny. And scanty, I've no doubt. Will that be all, Mr. Fraser?"

"Synthetic fibers," Alan mused when she had gone. "All available land needed for food, not natural fibers. And no tobacco."

"Not a pretty picture," Lee said. "What about war?"

"No war. The Chinese — Sinoasians, rather — will only be concerned about finding living room for their exploding population. War would mean atomic weapons and vast stretches of land made useless by radioactivity. Conventional weapons will only be used for routine police work, and so won't be developed to any great extent. The Sinoasians won't risk a war with ordinary weapons in case it leads to atomic ones. So it'll be a continuation of the present war on nerves, probably with added refinements."

"Cloak and dagger stuff on a grand scale," Lee supplied in a thoughtful tone. "Brainwashing and the rest of it. Good clean fun. . . . You're leaving me behind, old son. You don't need my help. You can think up enough horrors on your own."

"I'm just slipping down to the shop," Mrs. Low broke in from the door. She wore an unnecessary black coat and carried a basket over one arm. Nodding, Alan remembered to pass on Mr. Tarvin's message. Lee glanced at his watch and came to his feet.

"I didn't realize it was that time. My better half is under the impression I'm slaving away in the studio. With a bit of luck I should be able to make an unobtrusive way to my garret."

He made a small ceremony of bowing in the housekeeper's direction.

"May I offer you the pleasure of my company as far as the gate?"

And outside, when they reached the white-painted gate, he said — no banter now, no smile, only coldness. "Don't hurry back. Leave him alone in the house for a time. I'll keep an eye on things."

She nodded, replying formally: "Very good, Mr. Craig."

Inside his house, instead of going upstairs, Lee went into the lounge where Sybil sat in an easy chair, hands crossed placidly in her lap.

"Is it all right now?" she asked.

"I think so." He took out his cigarettes, looked at them and then returned the package unopened to his pocket. "Crowther seems satisfied. For what that's worth. . . . He admitted he'd underestimated ingrained instinct. Mrs. Low's gone out. Alan's alone in the house now." He rubbed the side of his nose. "If Crowther's done his work properly, this could be the start."

Alan finished typing the rough notes he had made during his talk with Lee. He felt grateful for the help Lee had given. Only one thing was needed now before he started work on the book. The name for the main character — and for the title — would have to be distinctive and descriptive. Forceful, Lee had suggested. He mouthed experimental syllables. None of the combinations had the right sound.

So he took the problem into the open, walking slowly down the drive, absently plucking a feather of forget-me-not, holding it between his fingers when he rested his arms on the gate.

Major Holt was stumping along the lane on his daily route march. From his cottage to the post office, back all the way to the farm, back again to his cottage. Two miles exactly, he had once told Alan, for he had paced the distance with military precision. Alan wondered why he didn't rid himself of the thick tweed jacket for summer, substituting a lighter, linen affair.

He suggested that when the marcher came abreast. The Major stopped, fingering the lapel thoughtfully.

"Something lighter," he grunted. "Linen. Eh?"

"It would be much more comfortable on a day like today."

"Worth considering," said the Major, and made a big thing of consulting his watch.

Alan took the hint. "Don't let me interrupt your schedule."

The other resumed his head-up, shoulders-back strut. As far as the post office. Halt. About face. Then back again.

Then back again . . .

And the odd little something that had been worry-nagging at the back of Alan's mind suddenly broke out into the open.

There had been this morning, and he had come along the passage and had forgotten which way to turn for his study. But that wasn't the something itself, only a link. The link was there because it was to do with going in wrong directions. Or coming from the wrong direction.

He had lain on his bed waiting for the sound of the doctor's car. When he had heard it he had looked through the window and its bonnet had been pointing toward Cradhill, not away from it, as it should have been. Dr. Crowther had only the one patient in Bewdey, so he couldn't have been to see anyone else first. In any case, he hadn't driven past before because there had been no earlier sound of his car.

A loss of sense of direction in the house in which he had lived all his life. A van that had disappeared. And now this. All on the same day when up until now every day had been a carbon copy of the one before.

Alan's involuntary contracting fingers crushed the flower spray to shreds. Shivering, he turned to make his way back inside. In the study he stood by the window looking at the back garden without seeing it. Dr. Crowther's solution to the van mystery could apply to the rest. But that was an explanation he rejected. He felt sure that he would be aware of even a momentary blackout. Thinking about it didn't help. He went to the desk and sat down.

Work. There was a novel to be written. But first — he still had to find a name for his character. It seemed strange that Lee hadn't offered any suggestions. Coming back to his feet again, Alan prowled the room in search of inspiration. Over the bureau Mrs. Low had tacked a cardboard wallet, designed to hold letters, supplied by one of the Cradhill tradesmen. "Wilfred Hagan. Family Butcher." "Wilfred"— no. But "Hagan" sounded more promising. Tucking the name away he wandered into the hall.

The barometer had been made by "Tibbet & Markson." "Markson?" "Hagan Markson?" The sound was satisfying, but not the one he was after. He went into the kitchen. A calendar was pinned to the front of the cabinet, "1966" above a bowl of roses. Supplied by another shop. "Arnold Smith & Co. Cradhill." "Arnold Hagan?" Still not the right feel. "Hagan Arnold" then, and the syllables slotted together as if they had been made for each other, as if he had had the name waiting at the back of his mind all the time.

Hagan Arnold it would be, and now a description to match the name.

And it seemed that he had also had the description waiting at the back of his mind all the time, the door unlocked now with the key of the name. Hagan Arnold came to life, so vividly that Alan could picture him standing there in the sun-filled kitchen, the light touching his dark hair, his teeth very white against bronzed skin, eyes slightly aslant, body slim and rakish and filled with latent power.

There was even a murmur of sound about the picture, an echo of words just this moment spoken, an echo that was taken up and lost in the real sound of the front door opening and Mrs. Low's voice calling — as it always did when she had been out —"It's only me, Mr. Fraser."

But the image of Hagan Arnold wasn't shattered. His smiling slanting eyes, his teeth, even the sound of his voice stayed in Alan's mind.

Lee looked in after tea.

"The opening of the novel all worked out in my mind," Alan told him. "I'll start getting it down on paper tomorrow." He didn't mention the name he had invented, willing the other to ask about it so that he could triumphantly produce it. He was disappointed when Lee didn't. But there was always another day.

And then, because he always told Lee about things that worried him, he spoke of Dr. Crowther's car, saying that there must have been another of the new momentary blackouts.

"Not this time," Lee said after a small hesitation. "I was waiting for the doc so I could tell him about this morning. He came up the lane from Cradhill, saw that my gates were open, turned into my drive and reversed there and then. It must have happened while you were getting from bed to window. No blackout that time, old son."

A reasonable explanation.

Undressing for bed that night was a series of automatic actions. Fragments of descriptions, snatches of conversation jostled in Alan's mind. Hagan Arnold, wearing a strange suit of shabby blue cloth, looking down at a muddy, slow-moving river. Hagan Arnold, gun in hand, pressed into the shadows of a dark alleyway. . . .

On the bedside table was the glass containing his sleeping draught that Mrs. Low had put ready as she always did. After buttoning his pajamas Alan picked it up and took it over to the window. The sun had dipped behind the hills. A thread of blue smoke trailed into the sky. It would be coming from the Major's cottage. He was the only one — blood thinned from a lifetime in the tropics — to need a fire at this time of year.

Constable Cowen pedaled along the lane on his heavy bicycle, the slanting light glinting on the white metal of uniform badges and buttons. Glancing upward as he labored by he nodded his helmeted head, and Alan, holding the curtain aside with one hand, had to set down the glass to acknowledge the greeting. And afterward he returned empty-handed to his bed, sliding between the cool sheets, completely forgetful of the untouched glass on the window ledge.

One moment he was lying awake, thinking of Hagan Arnold. And the next — so it seemed — he was wide awake again, only now to velvet blackness, the room filled with a strange humming sound.

Wide awake, the sound throbbing in his ears, he threw the sheets aside and padded to the window. The valley was dark. The sound seemed to come from the sky rather than from the valley. From the sky in the direction of the old farm. He leaned out. A star seemed to move, he couldn't be certain. Then the drumming faded and the night was silent. After a while he returned to his bed. And when morning came, with Lee joining him in the kitchen for the usual cup of coffee:

"A noise in the night?" Lee shook his head. "No — we didn't hear anything. You sure you weren't dreaming?"

"I don't dream very often," Alan said. "But I did last night. I wasn't dreaming when I heard the sound though. It seemed to come from the direction of the farm."

Lee had an explanation.

"A car, most likely, out on the Cradhill road. What you heard was the echo thrown back by the hills. What did you dream about, if it's not a personal question?"

34

"I can't remember." Alan looked at the door from behind which came the sounds of Mrs. Low busy with the vacuum cleaner. "I forgot to take my sleeping draught. I emptied it down the washbowl this morning."

Lee grinned. "Your secret is safe with me. But I shouldn't forget again. Mind if I help myself to more coffee?"

"Go ahead," Alan told him, and the phone in the hall gave two sharp rings. The cleaner stopped and there was the faint murmur of Mrs. Low's voice.

"An early caller," Lee remarked. Mrs. Low opened the door. Her face was puzzled; she spoke to Alan, but her words seemed directed to Lee.

"There was no one there. At least there was — I could hear breathing — but they just rang off without speaking."

"Odd." Lee set his cup down with careful deliberation. There was a short silence. Then: "Wrong number," he offered. "Peter Clamp getting his switches mixed up."

"Yes," Mrs. Low agreed vaguely, and came into the room to give Alan a letter. "This came for you, Mr. Fraser, just before the phone rang." She returned to her work.

The letter was from Kitch. He was sorry to say that two of Alan's stories had been rejected. But the bad news was tempered with brighter. The publishers lined up for the novel were prepared to pay an advance upon sight of a synopsis. Kitch suggested that he write a synopsis as soon as possible, highlighting only the more important parts. Alan passed the letter to Lee.

"Two stories flopped," Lee said. "Is that bad?"

"I was relying upon those to keep things going while I tackled the novel."

"No sell, no eat. You work pretty near the margin?"

"More or less hand to mouth," Alan said bleakly. "An advance from the publishers would save the day though. It means I'll have to really get down to it." He shook his head. "Quite a bit of thinking to be done first —"

"A stroll in the sunshine gathering inspiration?"

Alan looked through the window at the temptation of a cloudless sky. This had been another morning without mist on the hills. The weather could change very quickly.

"A stroll first," he agreed. "Then work."

He turned his face in the direction of the old farm. It occurred to him as he set off that he still hadn't told Lee that he had found a name for his character. He hadn't even set it down on paper.

The door of the Major's cottage was open, but there was no sign of the occupant. The garden of Clove Cottage, next door, was an eyesore of weeds. The place had stood empty for a long time. Alan glanced back over his shoulder, but he was earlier than usual this morning, too early for Fred's van to come trundling into view.

Outside his cottage, Tony Verity, coffee-colored hair uncombed, thick lips pursed in a soundless whistle, dark face preoccupied, spread a shirt to dry on his privet hedge. Alan paused for a brief interchange of pleasantries before moving on.

When he reached the gates of the farm he rested his arms along the top of them and stared at the deserted buildings. The sound in the night seemed to have come from here. It could have been, as Lee had suggested, the echo of a car on the Cradhill road. On the other hand . . .

He stooped to inspect the rusty padlock. And a voice behind him said: "Good morning, Mr. Fraser. Looks as if we're in for another fine day."

Alan swung round guiltily. Constable Cowen propped his bicycle against the hedge and came toward him, rubbing his large red hands together.

Alan found his voice. "Another fine day," he echoed.

"Out for your morning walk." The constable fingered the gray bristles of his upper lip. "If you're on your way back I'll walk part of the way with you."

They parted at the police cottage and Alan went the rest of the way alone. Reaching home he went into the study. Through the window he could see Mrs. Low hanging washing on the line, fighting a sheet and a sudden breeze. The telephone rang and he went into the hall to pick up the receiver.

"Alan Fraser here."

There was a short silence. And then a voice, a faraway voice said: "Is Hagan Arnold there?"

Alan stared at the receiver. For a moment there was no meaning to the words. Then came the shocking realization that it was impossible for anyone to know that name, that it existed only in his own imagination.

A black circle spun into being, racing toward him, growing, blotting out the sunlit hall, enveloping him, carrying him away with it.

3

SHIRT-SLEEVED, his jacket over his arm, Crowther came down the stairs, the treads creaking beneath his deliberate steps. In the study Lee's narrow face asked a silent question.

Crowther shook his head. "He's still out. I left Mrs. Low with him. I don't like it at all."

"Can't you give him anything?"

"Not if I can possibly avoid it. He's pumped full of dope already." The doctor eased his bulk wearily into a chair. "You'd better tell me what happened."

Lee used short sentences. "He was out for his walk. She was in the garden — didn't even know he'd returned. When she came back in the house he was lying on the hall floor. The telephone receiver was off its hook. She came for me, I called you then carried him upstairs."

Crowther's eyes widened. "The phone?"

"Looks like it. Another thing — it rang earlier. Mrs. Low answered, but whoever it was rang off without speaking. Clamp had brought a letter only a minute before the phone rang. Which means the switchboard was unattended."

"I don't like it," the other said again, but in a different voice. "We can't hold a p.m. until Alan comes round. He's shown no signs of becoming secretive?"

"None."

"Any reaction to Kitch's letter?"

"He reacted all right." Lee rubbed his nose. "He hasn't started writing yet, though. I've been through his papers. He was alone in the house for about an hour. I was hoping he might have come up with the name then. Apparently he didn't."

Crowther consulted his watch. "He's been unconscious long enough. I'd better go and see if I can bring him round now."

"You're a nice one," Lee said genially, "giving us all a shock like that. How do you feel now?"

Alan lay propped against the pillows, his white shirt only a shade paler than his face. His smile wasn't very convincing.

"A bit washed out. I'm sorry about all the fuss."

Lee sat sideways on the edge of the bed.

"I had a word with Crowther before he left. He told me he'd explained it all to you."

"More or less," Alan said doubtfully.

"A combination of three things; a disturbed night's sleep, a fault on the telephone switchboard, and your over-developed writer's imagination. You figured out a name for your character — what is it, by the way?"

"Hagan Arnold."

"Like 2016, it has a ring. A good name. All right, you get the name and you're so pleased with yourself that it stays at the forefront of your mind. And pops up at the first opportunity. Which was the phone ringing with no one at the other end. The sooner you get working on your novel and get the name out of your system, the better. Did Crowther say when you can get up?"

"Whenever I feel like it," Alan said.

The paper in the typewriter was still blank. Thoughts refused to change into words. But the opening paragraph, as Alan knew from experience, was always the hardest to write. He lighted a second cigarette from the stub of the first, came to his feet and wandered into the hall and then out through the front door.

Lee's face appeared over the hedge.

"That's more like it," he observed. "Out and about again with the minimum of delay. So long as you don't overdo things." He had a trowel in the hand that rested on the hedge. "Weeding," he explained. I take it you're thinking of taking another walk?"

"To help me think," Alan said. A flicker of blue could have been Sybil moving away from the inside of her window. When he started toward the gate Lee kept pace with him on his side of the hedge, talking about nothing in particular. And for the first time in his life Alan found himself anxious to get away from his next-door neighbor. But when he reached the gate and opened it Lee was there too, still talking, even laying his hand on Alan's arm so that it would have been sheer boorishness to have shaken it off.

A distant mutter of sound that grew into a roar was the little green van rocking into sight, braking, tires squealing, to come to a shuddering halt.

Fred Tolley leaned out, grinning. "Sorry about disturbing your rural sanctity. Blame old Tarvin. An urgent call for forgotten groceries. How are you this morning, Mr. Fraser? I missed you on my usual run."

Oddly, Alan found himself relaxing. Completely at ease he returned Fred's companionable grin.

"Enjoying the sunshine," he said.

"And the best of luck." Fred glanced up at his driving mirror. "More company on the way. Cheerful Peter Clamp. A smile and a cheery word for everyone. Didn't even bother to answer when I passed the time of day with him a few minutes ago. I'll leave you to it."

Still grinning he turned back to the wheel. The van chugged away and Peter Clamp, a somber, unsmiling figure in funereal black, thin dark hair centrally parted and plastered down, stopped when he reached the gate.

"Good morning, Mr. Fraser." He dealt words like cards from a pack. "A pleasant morning. I must apologize for the inconvenience caused by a fault on my switchboard."

Lee had slipped away. Alan found himself walking alongside the taciturn postmaster.

A strained silence lasted as far as the Major's cottage.

"Here we must part," Clamp said to Alan's relief. "My purpose in coming was to also apologize to Major Holt for any inconvenience caused."

Tony Verity was just emerging from his cottage.

"The muse has deserted me," he explained. "I seek solace in communing with nature."

They walked on together, Verity glibly voluble about the problems that beset artists, the juxtapositioning of colors, the canvas manifestations of abstract shapes, all of which Alan found incomprehensible and boring.

A short distance beyond Tarvin's shop was the stile that led to the hill path that Alan, for a change, had decided to take. He had hoped that his companion would leave him there, but instead Verity climbed the stile in his wake, beaming, expressing the enthusiastic opinion that a walk in the hills could be just the thing. . . .

The path meandered through a shady avenue of trees and emerged into the sunlight again, climbing steeply into the folds of bracken and heather slopes, with the lane and the cottages now hidden from view.

After a while, with Alan's legs starting to ache with the unaccustomed exercise, they retraced their steps. As they parted at Verity's cottage Constable Cowen came round the corner, slowing the pace of his bicycle to match Alan's step. At his own gate, Alan watched him cycle slowly away to disappear round the corner.

The whole idea about the walk was to allow him to be alone, to be able to think without fear of interruption. But he hadn't been left alone. It almost seemed — and this he found an almost frightening thought — that he had been subjected to a deliberate series of escorts. But that could have been coincidence. Fred could have happened along purely by chance to delay him while Peter Clamp came up. Verity could have been coming out of his cottage just at the moment Peter Clamp left him, again only by chance. And Constable Cowen — he was always up and down the lane. . . .

The phone rang as he opened the front door, but Mrs. Low, bustling, was there to answer it. He slipped by her and into the study. Coincidence? Or deliberately planned? And if planned — then why? In case he had another blackout? There was one way he could find out, set his mind at ease. Another walk. After lunch he would slip out of the house without either Mrs. Low or Lee seeing him leave. If he was being watched, then one of them would appear to walk with him.

"I'm just slipping down to the post office," Mrs. Low said from the door. She was struggling into her coat. "I'll only be away a few minutes."

She slammed the front door behind her with unusual violence.

Alan sat to the desk. The empty piece of paper was still in the typewriter. He rested his fingers on the keys. The phone rang, the sound echoing eerily. He sat back, staring toward the window. It rang again, and he had to force himself to go to answer it.

The same voice, the same muffled, faraway voice as before.

"Is Hagan Arnold there?"

His fingers tightened on the receiver. Whatever the voice was, it wasn't a hallucination. He was hearing it with his ears, not his mind.

"Who is that speaking?" he asked with an effort.

"This is Gregory Gallea," it said, and the line went dead.

Alan slowly replaced the receiver. Gregory Gallea. . . . He mouthed the words silently. He had never heard them before, and yet they were familiar. Like Hagan Arnold, when he had assembled that from names taken at random, the name Gregory Gallea slotted into his mind as if there had been a place waiting to receive it.

"Anyone home?" Lee's voice called from the kitchen.

Three quick strides and Alan was back in his study.

"In here," he called back, and was seated at the desk when Lee came in.

"I see you're at it," he said pleasantly. "Nose to the grindstone." He yawned noisily. "Had lunch yet?"

"Not yet. Mrs. Low's just slipped out."

"So she has. I met her on her way out and she mentioned something about Peter Clamp wanting to see her urgently about her pension."

"I've come up with a name for another of my characters," Alan said abruptly, watching Lee's face. "Gregory Gallea."

The lean features showed nothing beyond an assessing narrowing of the eyes.

"Quite a good one." And nothing in the tone other than interest. "You have the gift of being able to choose names that sound right. And what part is Mr. Gallea destined to play in the opus?"

"I haven't decided yet," Alan said.

Back in his own house, Lee picked up the phone. His voice was cold and curt.

"Clamp? Craig. I've talked with Mrs. Low. Put me through to Crowther. And you'd better listen in."

While he waited, frowning, drumming his fingers impatiently on the wall, Sybil came into the hall.

"Is something wrong?" she asked at sight of his face.

"Plenty." Motioning her to his side he spoke into the phone. "Crowther? Craig here. Our anonymous friend has shown his hand again. A while back Mrs. Low answered the phone. The man at the other end identified himself as Clamp, saying there was something he had to tell her, but he couldn't risk saying it over the phone. It stank, but she couldn't risk ignoring it. I kept my eye on things while she was away. Clamp wasn't at the office. She met him on her way back, and he told her he hadn't been responsible for the call."

"Go on," Crowther said steadily.

"I gave it about five minutes before going in to Alan. I didn't want to seem too obvious — he's getting perceptive. Nothing happened while I was with him."

"But five minutes unaccounted for. He said nothing?"

"No," Lee said. "Is the p.m. slipping?"

"No," Crowther said. "No." But he didn't sound too certain. He added: "Our friend has to be someone here in the village."

"I'd figured that out for myself," Lee said softly. "Does the name 'Gregory Gallea' mean anything to you?"

"Not offhand. Should it?"

"He came up with it from somewhere."

"I'll check with my people," Crowther said. "No doubt you will be doing the same. Is that all?"

"Yes," Lee snapped, and rang off. "You heard all that?" he asked Sybil.

She nodded, white teeth biting on her bottom lip. "I suppose it has to be one of us here in the valley who is responsible for the phone calls?"

"It's one of us all right. If an outsider had managed to find a way in — which is virtually impossible — he wouldn't have a snowball's chance in hell of remaining hidden. Apart from anything else the necessities of life would bring him into the open."

"Not Clamp," she mused. "He's in the clear. And Mrs. Low. Verity and Holt were with Tarvin at his place at the time of the first call. That leaves —" She wrinkled her forehead.

"Not counting you and me," Lee supplied, "three. Tolley, Cowen, and Crowther." He smiled coldly at her exclamation. "There is no reason why Crowther should be as inviolate as Caesar's wife."

"There we are," Dr. Crowther said, heavily benign. "That's all for today." He returned the hypodermic syringe to its metal case. "Did you remember to have a rest after lunch?"

"Yes." Alan rolled down his shirt sleeve.

"Good. And you're taking the tablets regularly."

"I take care of that, Doctor," Mrs. Low said from the door. She stepped aside. "I'll see you out, Doctor."

Alan lowered himself to the chair. His arm still stung from the injection and he rubbed it absently. The feeling of torpidity was fading, as it always did, to be replaced by a sense of well-being. After a while that would go too, and he would be normal again.

Normal . . .

He heard the engine throb as the car moved away, followed by the sound of the front door being closed. Then the stairs creaked. Mrs. Low going up to her room to change. In half an hour she would be down again, first with the afternoon tablets, then with tea. He went into the front room, looking through the net curtains without disturbing them. There was no sign of Lee, but Sybil was there, basket over one arm, snipping the heads from dead roses.

Walking quietly and quickly, filled with an odd kind of tense exhilaration, Alan went back along the passage, through the kitchen, and out into the back garden. Without pausing to look back he crossed the strip of lawn, pushed through a screen of bushes and came to the boundary privet hedge. Thrusting bodily through it he emerged on the springy turf of the lower slopes. Immediately ahead, perhaps a hundred yards away, was a copse of heavy-leafed trees. He made toward them at a half-run, crouching, turning for a brief inspection of the houses when he reached the outer fringe of scrub.

The cool and shade of a miniature glade — thick moss underfoot — and then he was out in the sunlight again, climbing over slippery grass, making his way upward between clumps of heather and gorse toward the faint line of the hill path.

When he reached it, with the wind patting his face, with the houses out of sight, he slackened his pace, breathing heavily from the unusual exertion. He walked then, for quite some time. He chose a place where the ground was even and where tall bracken screened even the little-used path. There he lowered himself to the ground, lying flat on his back, one hand in front of his eyes against the sun's brilliance.

Perhaps he dozed — he was tired after the climb. He hadn't put on his watch and so had no way of telling how long he had been there when the girl came. He was sitting up when she came down the slope above, intent on finding her way through the vicious briar, stumbling a little and half-sliding, almost on top of him before glancing up, startled to see him there.

4

THE GIRL wore a loose white blouse of some silky material, sleeveless, buttoned high at the neck and with three small blue bows set in a vertical row on the left breast, an unusual decoration reminiscent of some kind of insignia. Tight, golden-brown corduroys were fastened above brown bare knees. The straps of her wooden-soled sandals were studded with brilliants.

A cloud of dark hair framed a pointed face. It was the irregularity of her features that made them attractive rather than pretty, only the wide gray eyes level, brows and mouth being set at a slant. Her figure was almost boyish, the blouse only hinting at the shapes beneath.

It was the jeweled sandal straps that drew his eyes. He had never seen any like them before. Seeing the direction of his gaze she grimaced, mistaking his interest.

"Not very sensible footwear for this sort of thing." She extended a slim leg, stooping to run rueful fingers along the red lines of briar scratches. "It's so long since I've been this way that I'd forgotten how rugged it was."

She lowered herself companionably to his

51

side, clasped her hands about her knees and sighed relief.

"I'd almost given up hope of finding somewhere to rest in this wilderness." She looked curiously about her. "I can't be all that far from the village?"

"About a mile," Alan told her. "You can't see the path from here — it's the other side of that rise."

"A mile?" She grimaced again. "Then I need time to get my breath back before tackling it." She smiled sunnily at him. "And what are you doing out here in the wilds?"

"I live down there." He nodded in the general direction of the village. "I just came out for a walk."

"So you're an inhabitant of Beecher's End." It wasn't a question.

"Beecher's End?" His surprise caused her brows to lift.

"You mean it isn't? Don't tell me I've lost my way!"

He smiled at her dismay. "It sounds as if you have. That's Bewdey down there."

"Bewdey?" She bit her lip. "Are you sure?" Then: "That's a silly thing to say. You know what I mean."

"I ought to be sure. I've lived there all my life."

"So that's that." She looked back over her shoulder. "So where did I lose my way?"

"You must have taken a completely wrong direction. I've never even heard of Beecher's End."

"You haven't?" She drew her brows together in a delicate frown of puzzlement. "That's odd. I mean, it can't be all that far away."

He pointed. "The valley is a dead end. The road runs along the bottom. The nearest place is Cradhill. About ten miles away."

"Cradhill?" Her frown deepened. "Another pocket-sized village?"

"A fair-sized market town," he corrected.

"Well —" She lapsed into silence. Alan's forehead was beginning to smart where the sun had caught it. When he reached up to rub the scars her gaze followed his fingers.

"To be quite honest," he told her, "it's more than ten years since I was in Cradhill. I can't recall very much about the place."

"Ten years?" she marveled.

"I never leave the valley," he said simply.

"What about your service?"

"Service?"

She laughed then, throwing back her head. "You are out of touch. You must have had exemption." Her eyes returned to the scars.

"I believe there were some papers," he said slowly, trying to remember. "Dr. Crowther probably took care of them. Or Lee — he's my neighbor. Lee Craig. My name's Alan Fraser."

"Well-met by sunlight," she returned lightly. "Karen Summer." She didn't offer her hand.

"Miss Summer?" he wondered, and again she threw back her head to laugh.

"That's one way of putting it, Alan. You

sound almost medieval. I'm not attached, certainly. And you?"

He shook his head. "No," accepting her humor without resentment.

"You don't live alone?"

"I have a housekeeper."

Her eyes widened. "In this day and age? And what do you do with yourself when you're not sunning yourself in the hills?"

"I write."

"You mean for a living? Books?"

He took out his cigarettes and offered them to her. "Short stories up until now. I've just started on my first novel."

"You write under your own name?" She took a cigarette, rolled it between her fingers, held it to her nose and then glanced up, eyes wide again. "You do yourself well —"

"I write under my own name." He flicked his lighter.

"I don't get much time for reading." She leaned back, luxuriously inhaling smoke. "I'm at the farm in the next valley. Or what I fancied was the next valley. I must sort out my bearings when I get back. They sent me there three months ago. I had six days owing so I thought I'd take them while the weather holds out.

"It isn't my first time in this part of the world. When I was at school I often used to spend the holidays with an uncle who lived in Beecher's End. He's dead now. Before I went into farming I served a term in the hospital service."

She reached across to touch the scars on

his forehead. "I know something about this sort of thing, Alan. That's why I treated you to a potted autobiography. So that you would know I was interested and not morbidly curious. What caused them?"

He looked down at his feet. "An accident."

"But you'd rather not talk about it?" She was contrite. "I'm sorry; I shouldn't have asked."

"It's not that —" He made a vague movement with his shoulders. "I can't remember very much about it. Which is just as well, I suppose. Partial amnesia plus other things. I was born here in Bewdey. Thirty-six years ago. I can't even remember what my parents were like. But from one of them I inherited a form of epilepsy called '*Petit mal.*'"

He waited for her nod of understanding. "I couldn't go to school in the normal way. My parents taught me at home, and Lee — we grew up together — helped as best he could. He still does."

"The accident was about ten years ago. A head-on car crash. My people were killed and I was badly burned."

"I thought they were graft scars," Karen said gently.

"I can't remember anything about the hospital. When it was over Mrs. Low brought me home. She was the nursemaid when I was a child and has stayed on ever since. I used to get bad blackouts. They're getting better now. But I can't travel any distance yet."

She rested her chin on her hands while

her eyes slowly traveled the length of the hills. From behind a screen of trees smoke curled lazily into the sky, the only sign of life.

"From the Major's cottage," Alan said absently. "He was in the tropics for a long time. About this time of day he has to light a fire."

Karen roused herself. "And what time of the day will it be?"

"He always lights up at five o'clock."

She unclasped her hands from round her knees. "Which means it's time I was starting the long trek back."

They started to scramble to their feet at the same time, Alan trying to be up first so that he could help her, but finding his legs had become cramped, so that she was up first and standing at the side of the small clearing by the time he had found his feet.

"Will I see you again, Karen?" he asked anxiously.

"Well. . ." She regarded him thoughtfully. "I was toying with the idea of having another try at finding Beecher's End tomorrow. But on second thought perhaps it's not such a good idea. Places change. They're never the same as you remember them."

"Bewdey never changes," Alan said. "Sometimes I wish it would."

"Don't wish that!" she cried fiercely, and then was repentant, her voice softening. "I almost said you don't know when you're well off. But that would have been cruel and stupid. You've had a bad time and things can't be all that happy now. But at least your present way of life is peaceful. There are people who would give anything to be able to change places with you. To be able to get lost in the hills and forget about the world outside. . . ."

She broke off, laughing a little. "See what an afternoon in the hills has done for me. Poetry bubbling to the surface." And then, suddenly serious again: "I'd sell my soul to be able to live in your valley."

The intensity of the declaration reduced him to silence. He found his voice again when she turned to go.

"But you will come back again tomorrow?"

Her smile was back. "If I can find my way." And at the expression on his face: "All right, Alan. Tomorrow afternoon. Earlier than today if I can get away."

He watched her go, turning to wave when she reached the crest, then he made his way to the path that led down to the lane.

And when he was out of sight the man who had been watching, concealed in a hollow, came stiffly to his feet, rubbing his legs before setting off in the opposite direction. Gregory Gallea smiled to himself as if well pleased with what he had seen and heard.

The lane, when Alan reached the stile, was empty in both directions. He walked slowly, his eyes on the rough surface of the lane, reliving his meeting with Karen. He remembered among other things, her surprise at the cigarette, as if it had been something out of the usual. And yet it had come from an ordinary packet bought from Tarvin's shop. He remembered the odd decoration of the three blue bows and the way she had laughed and seemed surprised when he had wanted to know if she was married. And he also remembered, with a shock of dismay, that although she had promised to come again tomorrow he hadn't thought to ask her at what time. But she had said something about trying to be earlier. . . .

The smarting on his forehead was hardening into a band of sullen pain. Pressure made the skin feel brittle and taut. For a moment the ground rocked under his feet and when he raised his head a momentary red-tinged blackness blotted out the sun. When it had gone he resumed walking. For Tony Verity, lounging over his gate, cigarette hanging from his loose mouth, he managed a smile and a few passing words.

The blackness came swooping again as he turned the corner. The lane dipped and rose sickeningly. Hands clasped to his burning forehead he staggered to the verge, lowering himself to the grassy bank. The last thing he remembered before the blackness became complete was Fred's green van chugging along the lane toward him.

Awareness started to return as he was being lifted out of the van outside his house. He identified voices as being those of Fred and Lee. There was a vague impression of being helped along the drive, arms beneath his shoulders.

And then the cool of the hall and a sudden darkness that was blinding after the sun-filtered mists of the outside. He was struggling against the terror of this new blackness, fighting restraining hands, managing to break free, staggering along the passage toward the oblong of light that was the open kitchen door.

Feet pounded in his wake. The kitchen was a confusion of shapes, only the back door, open wide, standing out clearly, a blaze of light that offered an escape from the terror of darkness. Then he was out in the open again, in the brightness, his face to the wall, his hands groping senselessly at the rough brickwork while he fought another losing battle against the menacing blackness.

As Lee came bursting from the doorway at his side his knees buckled and he slid to the ground. And on the wall above, where his head had been an instant earlier, an incandescent circle sprang into hissing, vicious being; a circle of writhing heat that shrivelled bricks and mortar and left in their place a steaming, glowing red-hot scar.

It was the following morning. Lee and Crowther were in the study that was filled with the first slanting light of a new day. The doctor, his large face a gray mask of tiredness, leaned back in his chair and closed his eyes.

Standing by the window, Lee asked: "How does he seem now?"

"I've done all I can. He should wake up at his usual time."

"It was sunstroke?"

"Heat delirium, yes. And something else." Crowther opened his eyes with an effort. "Something I don't understand. Some intrusion. There's a block that won't be moved. I had to neutralize it."

"From the phonecall?"

"No. I located and canceled that. And another one. During that five-minute gap. It came from someone calling himself Gregory Gallea."

"I thought that was where he got it from," Lee said. He frowned heavily. "It doesn't make sense. That attack came from the direction of the copse. I sent Tolley to see what he could find. Nothing. But it has to be one of us."

"That's your problem. With three varied incidents to work on you should be able to reach an answer by process of elimination."

"I know my job," Lee said frostily. "Elimination doesn't work. The only ones who could have made the phone calls were covered for the last incident."

"A stranger in our midst," Crowther hazarded. "How, I don't know. Smuggled in and kept hidden? Or perhaps there's a way in over the hills that was missed. It may be worthwhile doing another survey."

"That's being taken care of," Lee rejoined. "But there's no pattern. Two attempts to undermine the p.m. Then a deliberate attempt to kill. Different techniques."

60

Crowther asked coldly: "How did he manage to slip away unnoticed?"

"If your p.m. had remained fixed there would be no need for you to be asking that. I don't know how he managed it. But it was a deliberate attempt at evasion."

"The phone calls weakened the p.m.," the other retorted resentfully. "How long was he away?"

"There's no way of telling exactly. Verity was the first to see him. That was shortly after 17.30."

"Something happened while he was out there," Crowther said. "What, I don't know. It was blocked off. I had to neutralize it, which isn't a very clever thing to do." He raised a censorious eyebrow. "We mustn't have a repetition."

"I've already sent for an Erdam," Lee told him. "It will be here some time this morning."

"That will be all right so long as he stays in the open. A pity you didn't think of that before." The doctor stirred himself, yawned, glancing at his watch. "Seven. He should wake at nine. I'd better try to get some sleep in."

"And when he does wake?"

"Business as usual," Crowther said. "At least, I hope so."

It was a morning like any other. Sunlight flooded the bedroom with golden warmth. The mingled scents of coffee and bacon drifted from below. Alan yawned his con-

tented way to the bathroom. Washing
brought back memories of the previous day.
He dabbed carefully with the towel at the
tenderness of reddened forehead. For all the
discomfort of sunburn it had been a pleasant
walk. An uneventful one. One like any other.

Back in his bedroom he opened the wardrobe. Today, the blue blazer and light gray
slacks. And a silk scarf instead of a tie because of the soreness at the back of his neck.

And downstairs, in the kitchen, Mrs. Low
had his breakfast waiting, and Lee was
there, cup in hand, to indulge in the expected chaff about people who wandered in
the hills and got themselves burned for their
trouble. . . .

A day like any other.

In the study Alan changed the red rectangle of the calendar. In his diary he wrote
"Wednesday, June 15" ready for today's entry. For the next hour he typed busily, the
words flowing until the interruption of Mrs.
Low with the morning tablets. Then, the
train of thought broken, he idled to the window. Just for a moment, looking at the hills,
he had the feeling that something important
was hovering at the back of his mind, just a
fraction out of memory's reach.

Later, Mrs. Low brought coffee. "I suppose
you'll be taking your usual morning walk,
Mr. Fraser?"

"Yes." Then unaccountably he heard himself changing his mind. "No. I think I'll go
this afternoon instead."

Now he was alone with the knowledge that

there would be no more interruptions till lunch time. But inspiration had dried. He went out into the front garden. Apart from a dusting of feathery clouds the sky was clear. A heat haze shimmered on the hills. There was a smell of freshly cut privet — Lee busy with clippers on the dividing hedge.

"That's what I like to see," Alan observed contentedly.

"It's all right for you," Lee retorted equably. "No wife to keep your nose to the grindstone. No walk this morning?"

"This afternoon, for a change," Alan told him.

Lee broke off work to watch him return to the house. He frowned, scratching the side of his nose dangerously with the points of the shears.

After lunch, as usual, he rested, lying on top of the bed. Sleep refused to come, barred by the slow tumult of his thoughts. There had to be some reason why he had changed his mind on the spur of the moment, deciding to walk in the afternoon instead of the usual morning. And why he felt he had to take the hill path instead of the lane. It was only very rarely that he went up in the hills. He couldn't recall the last time. . . . Yesterday he had walked along the lane. It was impossible to get sunburned under the leafy shade of the trees that sheltered the narrow lane. And yet — his fingers touched the stiff flesh of his forehead — this.

He had been somewhere out of the shade,

where the sun burned. Not along the lane.
. . . He pressed his fingers to his temples,
trying to think, to remember.

After a while he went to the bathroom,
running water into the basin and cupping
coldness over his face. There were scratches
on the backs of his hands; he discovered
them when using the towel. He remembered
how they had come there. When he had
pushed through the hedge. When he had left
the house by the back way, unobserved, to
make his way up the hills. He had sat in a
clearing, and the girl had come. Karen. . . .

Downstairs again, in the study, he could
hear Mrs. Low busy in the kitchen. His
watch told him what point she had reached
in her unchangeable routine. There was the
sound of water draining from the sink. Alan
closed the study door, leaving an inch of
space through which he watched her bustling
along the passage, untying her apron as she
came, then up the stairs. He waited for the
thud of her bedroom door before making his
way through the spotless, sterile kitchen
and out into the garden.

His back to the door he paused, looking
about him. A circle of concrete on the wall
by his head was puzzling by its newness until
he remembered that there had been a lamp
there, that the iron bracket had worked loose
and been removed a few days ago.

And now it was a matter of repeating
yesterday's maneuver. There was no sign of
Lee or Sybil. Fifteen minutes later he had
reached the path, hidden now from the vil-

lage, and was following it, filled with a steadily growing feeling of anticipation and exhilaration.

And when he reached the clearing, the girl was there, wearing the same dress only now with calf-high white boots instead of the jeweled sandals. She was coming to her feet, smiling and trying to be mock-stern at the same time.

"I thought you'd forgotten, Alan. . . ."

"I had," he confessed, returning her smile. "At least, it was at the back of my mind all morning. I knew there was something. . . . Then it came to me."

"You forgot?" Then her smile was replaced with a sudden look of concern. "You had another blackout, Alan?"

"Not this time, Karen. Something more mundane. A touch of sunstroke. Dr. Crowther said it was quite a bad attack."

"Sunstroke? Then you shouldn't be standing out in the open like this." She looked about her. "We'd better go to the other side of that rise. It won't be so comfortable, but at least you'll be in the shade."

The wiry turf backing a granite outcrop sloped steeply. Sitting, they had to dig in their heels to stop from sliding. But it was pleasantly secluded and shady.

She touched his forehead with cool fingers. "I had the feeling that something like this must have happened. Only I thought it was something much worse. With the proof in front of me I have no option but to forgive you. I suppose you had to spend all yesterday in bed. I waited nearly two hours for you. It was only by chance — and my goodness of heart — that made me try again today." She broke off at his expression. "Is something wrong, Alan?"

"Yesterday?" His mouth was suddenly dry. "You said you came here yesterday, and I didn't come?" He put his hand to his forehead. "What day is it today?"

"Thursday," she told him, watching his face.

Yesterday had been Tuesday. This morning he had altered the calendar from Tuesday to Wednesday. In his diary there had only been the entry for Tuesday. Today had to be Wednesday.

She interpreted the look on his face. "You've lost a day." She touched his arm. "Don't worry. You must have slept right through."

That was the first explanation that had come to his mind. But it wasn't — couldn't be the answer.

"They would have said something — Lee, or Sybil, or Mrs. Low."

"You would have thought they would," Karen said slowly. And then: "But this doesn't make sense."

"No." He stared at her. "There are other things too. . . ."

Karen's eyes remained fixed to his face while he told her about Fred's van and the car that had pointed in the wrong direction.

About how he had to think to remember which door led to his study, and how part of him believed that a bracket-lamp had once hung at the back of the house, but that another part of his mind told him there had never been a lamp there at all, for all there was a circle of new concrete there now. He told her about the seemingly escorted walk.

She heard him out in silence. When he took out his cigarettes she accepted one without comment. But she was clearly deep in thought. He held out his lighter.

"And you've known"— she drew in smoke —"all these people all your life?"

"Most of them. All except Tony Verity and the Major. They came to Bewdey about ten years ago. The others have always been here."

"All very odd." She glanced sideways at him, eyes narrowed against smoke. "And there's something else that strikes me as being odd. Here's Bewdey — I think I've got it right — a couple of houses, three cottages — one empty — and a deserted farm. And to cater for the needs of how many people? — nine — including the shopkeepers themselves, there is a post office and a shop. Which doesn't make sense."

"I'd never thought about it that way before," Alan said slowly.

She came briskly to her feet. "I think I'd like to take a look at this village of yours, Alan. Is there some place where we can see without being seen?"

In the small room at the top of his house that he called a studio, Lee sat by the window that overlooked the back garden and the hills beyond. A slender metal tube projected through the upper part of the window. It was some six feet long, mounted on a tripod, with a cannister protuberance at the far end. Two sets of wires trailed from a similar protuberance at the end inside the room, one set leading to the padded earphones clamped to his head, the other to a small metal box with dials along its front. Lee revolved on his seat as he swung the tube to slowly traverse the line of hills.

"Not a murmur," he said to Sybil.

"He must be out there somewhere," she said. "He's nowhere else in the village. No one saw him go."

He motioned her sharply to silence. "Thought I caught something then. False alarm. For no one to see him leave means he must have deliberately sneaked away like he did the last time. Crowther's p.m. seems to be coming apart at the seams. I'll swear he's not alone up there. But if they've found themselves a hollow, with solid earth between, this wouldn't pick up a thing, even if they shouted at the tops of their voices."

"Are there many places like that?"

"A few." He hunched his shoulders impatiently. "See for yourself; the map's on the table. I did a quick survey. There's a couple of hollows near the fork. My guess is he's tucked away in one of those. But with whom?"

"Here we are," Alan said. "We should be able to see most of the valley from here. And if we keep our heads down we shouldn't be spotted." He wondered about, but didn't question, her reasons for not wanting to be observed.

Karen used both hands to part the brown-green fronds.

"My house is the far one of those two on the right," he told her.

She followed the direction of his gaze without speaking. After a few moments she let the fronds fall back into place and sat back on her heels.

"The Major lives in the end one of the three cottages that were just ahead," Alan said when she remained silent. "Tony Verity in the one at the other end."

"Yes," Karen said, and then she started speaking quickly, in a monotone, almost breathlessly, the words tumbling over one another.

"The last time I was here — eight years ago — those two houses weren't there. At least not like they are now — they were just a couple of tumble-down cottages that had been empty for ages. And the cottage where you say the Major has lived for ten years. That used to belong to my uncle. That's where I used to stay. He lived there right up to the time of his death. And he died last year."

There was a silence.

"This isn't Bewdey," Karen said. "This is Beecher's End."

5

THIS WAS BEWDEY, Alan's thoughts drummed almost hypnotically. This was Bewdey where he had been born and lived all his life. It could never be anywhere else. This was Bewdey. Karen was mistaken. Seen from a distance one village must look very like another. She was mistaken. This was Bewdey, not Beecher's End.

They had returned to the shade of the hollow again.

Karen said earnestly: "I know what you must be thinking, Alan. But I've not made a mistake. I know it sounds impossible, but this is Beecher's End. You must believe that."

She paused. "I had to tell you. I think I guessed from the start. . . . I had to tell you and get it over and done with. Something's very wrong. If I'm to try to help you sort it out, and I'd like to try, then I have to tell you the truth."

He found a voice that he didn't recognize as his own. "This is Bewdey. I was born here. I've always lived here."

"Look at me, Alan!" She set her hands on his shoulders, forcing him round until he was looking at her. "Now listen and try to under-

70

stand. The village down there is Beecher's End. For some reason someone has altered the place a little and changed its name to Bewdey. I know it like the palm of my hand. I know every cottage, every garden. But not the hills — they stretch for miles. Uncle would never let me come up here in case I got lost. But down there —"

Alan buried his face in his hands. He could barely hear her through the thunder tumult in his mind.

"I don't know whether I am doing right," Karen said helplessly. "All I know is that something is very wrong — something monstrous and unnatural — and you are right in the middle. Scenery on a stage; cardboard cottages filled with sawdust people. But why — ?"

The thunder was receding, the tension easing. Alan lifted his face from his hands. His mind was starting to function again, but now he had the strange feeling of being two separate identities, one rebelling against the things Karen was saying, the other accepting them.

"How are you feeling now?" she asked anxiously.

"Like something had exploded inside my head leaving everything numbed. It's sorting itself out now."

She sighed relief. "You've weathered it better than I thought. May I have a cigarette, Alan?"

He found satisfaction in his ability to cope with the commonplace actions of taking out his case and opening it. And his hand, he discovered when he flicked the lighter, was almost steady.

"That's better." She leaned back, drawing deeply on the cigarette. "I needed that." She gazed reflectively at him for a few moments. "This isn't Bewdey. Can you accept that?"

He nodded slowly. "I can't believe it. But I have to accept it."

"I've never come across anything remotely like this before. Even when I was working in the hospital. So what do we do? Do we leave things as they are, in case tampering with them does more harm than good? Or do we try to find the reason?"

"I don't know," Alan said. "I just don't know. I need time to think." He turned to look in the direction of the village. "If I wasn't born in that house down there, where did I come from? And who am I? Am I Alan Fraser?"

"Where do we start?" She touched his scars. "These. These are real. They look very recent to me, but it's hard to tell. But it means that at some time you must have been in an accident. We could try to find out about that. Hospital records — there's bound to be a record somewhere. And there's something else we could work on. You say you are a writer. Have you ever seen any of your stories in print?"

He tried to think. "I can't remember."

"If you had seen them," she said wisely, "you'd remember. How do you sell them?"

"Through a literary agent called Eric Kitch. His office is in Cradhill."

"And that's another thing," Karen said. "I'm certain there's no such place as Cradhill. Otherwise I'd have heard of it. Have you ever met this Eric Kitch?"

"No," Alan said. "At least, not that I can recall."

"You write the stories, send them to him, and he sends you the money for them?"

"More or less. Sometimes they're rejected."

"Dead end," she said evenly. "So what do we talk about now?" She glanced at him quickly. "How are you weathering the storm now, Alan?"

"Part of me is still numbed." He closed his eyes. "There's a feeling — inside my head, I think — of two separate things. It's hard to explain. Part of me knows that this is Bewdey. The other part knows it isn't." He opened his eyes again. "I'm not even making sense to myself. What is happening, Karen? If this isn't Bewdey; if I haven't lived here all my life — where did I come from? Who was I before I was Alan Fraser?"

"Steady, Alan." She laid her hand on his arm at the anguish in his voice. "I may be doing wrong but I want to help you all I can. There's nothing to go on, though, except your scars. You could have lost your memory after the accident that caused them. I've had a lot to do with amnesia. Usually the memory comes back gradually. Sometimes a shock will bring it back. In rare cases it never comes back at all. In a case like that it may be possible for an artificial past to be planted in place of the missing real one. That could have happened to you, but I don't think it did. An ordinary total amnesiac would simply be returned to his family to start life afresh. But that hasn't happened to you, which means you must be something special. I think your real past was deliberately obliterated. Brainwashed. Have you heard of that sort of thing?"

"No," he said.

"The fact that you don't know what brainwashing is," Karen said slowly, "could prove that I'm right. Outside, in the world outside this valley, every man and woman in the street knows what it is. But it isn't part of your knowledge. So it's something they don't want you to know about. Or am I making something out of nothing?" She drew a deep breath. "Let's stick to facts. You may have been a writer before the accident. But let's assume you weren't. I have the feeling you're not a literary type. So they made you a writer for a special purpose. Do they tell you what to write?"

"No," Alan told her, and then hesitated, remembering Lee and his suggestions for the novel. And remembering too how everyone else in the place seemed interested in the novel.

"You're not certain?" she asked, watching his face closely.

"I've just started on a novel. My first. The

rough ideas were in my mind — I'd even made notes. But Lee —"

"He told you what it was to be about?"

"Not in so many words. But he tried to help. He suggested it be a fictional autobiography —"

Karen sat up. "The story of someone's life. We may be on to something. Whose life, Alan?"

He shook his head. "No one in particular. It took me a long time to even invent a name for the character."

"And you came up with — ?"

"Hagan Arnold."

"Hagan Arnold." She shook her head. "It doesn't mean anything."

"It wouldn't. I simply went round the house choosing names at random. One from a calendar, I think it was, the other from a wallet affair — the sort of thing shopkeepers turn out."

"Cradhill shopkeepers?" she asked steadily.

"That's right. One was a butcher, the other. . . ." Then he understood the expression on her face. "But there's no such place as Cradhill —"

"No." She was quietly triumphant. "They offered you a small selection of names. Like a stage magician with a pack of cards. You told them which names you had picked?"

He nodded. "Yes."

"Were they happy about them?"

He remembered Lee's approval. "Yes."

"Then Hagan Arnold must be a real person," she said with an odd air of certainty. "Perhaps someone you once knew, perhaps even you yourself. Are you positive you'd never heard the name before?"

"Yes," he said, and then stopped. Somewhere at the back of his mind ideas revolved, trying to break through the mists of memory. Something to do with a telephone. . . . But while he fought to draw the curtain aside a thought occurred to him.

"Hagan Arnold can't be a real person," he said simply. "My novel is set fifty years in the future. In my story, Hagan Arnold hasn't even been born yet."

Karen leaned back again. "So that's that." Her tone revealed disappointment. "A second dead end. I had the bright idea that you had information of some kind tucked away in your mind, and getting you to write about it was one way of bringing it out. But having you write about what you think may happen in fifty years' time can't be of any use to anyone. It has to be pure fiction. Just guesswork. Now I'm stumped completely." She sat up suddenly, looking about her. "How long have we been talking? Have you any idea of the time, Alan?"

This time he had his watch. "Almost five-thirty."

Just for an instant a brief flicker of puzzlement passed across her oval features. Then: "I'm afraid I'll have to go."

"But I will see you again?" His anxiety was almost childlike.

She touched his cheek lightly. "I've still got three days of freedom left. And having started all this I can't leave you in the lurch. I'll be back again tomorrow." She smiled at him. "Same time, same place."

On his feet first he held out his hand to help her up, and when she was standing at his side, he turned to look toward the village.

"It's not going to be easy for you now," she said, interpreting his gaze. "There's not much I can say to help. For the time being you'll have to pretend that you haven't discovered the truth. You've got to play their game. . . . Try to act naturally. Keep your eyes and ears open." She touched his face again. "Now I must go."

He walked back the way he had come, slowly, feet dragging. There was the same uncanny feeling of being two separate personalities. Two different people conflicting inside his mind. And too there was the dread of having to face Them. The people he lived amongst. Lee, Mrs. Low, Dr. Crowther.

"They'll know something has happened," he said aloud for the comfort of hearing his own voice.

"Not if you keep your wits about you," a second, silent voice said inside his head.

Bees droned amongst the gorse. Ferns stirred to a breeze. There was the muted sound of a car coming from the direction of the road, not the splutter of the van, but the steady hum of Dr. Crowther's sedan.

"They'll ask me where I've been," Alan told the empty path.

"Tell them you've been for a walk while you thought about the novel," whispered the silent voice.

He reached the place where he had to leave the path and make his way down through the copse to the house. Through a gap in the trees he could see the open back door and alongside, the new gray circle of concrete, raw-ugly against the surrounding brickwork.

"There never was a lamp there," said the second voice. *"There's no such place as Cradhill. Where does Fred Tolley come from? And Dr. Crowther? Where does the road lead to?"*

There's no time to find out now, Alan thought. I've been away too long already.

"There may not be another chance," insinuated the voice.

The path curved away from the road in a wide horseshoe loop. He cut across the brow of the hill to save time, meeting up with it again some distance beyond the houses. Through the trees he caught a glimpse of the isolated post office. Through a second gap the road was a twisting gray ribbon winding away out of sight.

He left the path where the trees grew close together, a leafy barrier between hills and road. There was a break between them, a smooth emerald avenue that led to a gate giving access to the road. And Fred Tolley's little green van was there tucked away in a small clearing, hidden from both road and path. Looking about him he found oil marks where a second vehicle — and he knew whose that would be — had been parked.

Opening the gate he stepped out into the road. Half a mile farther along it ended. There was a line of broken tarmac, and then nothing but piles of rubble and tangled dead branches, heaped high, hiding what lay behind and completely blocking the way.

"That's Crowther's car," Sybil said.

Lee, headphones clipped to his ears, both hands guiding the projecting tube, spoke without turning. "Tell him to come up here."

He leaned back when Crowther came in.

"He gave us the slip about two hours ago. But there wasn't a whisper till twenty minutes ago." He reached to thumb a switch on the metal box. An amplifier hummed and Alan's voice filled the room.

"They'll know something has happened."

"Is that all?" Crowther asked.

"Five minutes later," Lee adjusted a dial, "— this."

"They'll ask me where I've been," said Alan's voice.

Lee shrugged. "And that's all."

"He must be alone," Sybil said. "No replies. Talking to himself."

"Where did you first pick him up?" Crowther asked sharply.

"C.16," Lee told him. "And the second one, C.19."

"He's making his way back along the top path," Sybil interpreted, bending over the map. "C.19 is almost directly ahead. But that was thirty minutes ago. He should have been back by now."

"Still nothing?" Crowther asked, one hand on Lee's shoulder.

"Not a bloody murmur. This thing has a range of two miles. He's alone all right."

Crowther straightened, fingering the fleshy roll under his chin.

"This is the second time you've let him slip through your hands," he observed in a colorless voice. "It won't look good on the report."

"Your p.m. is as full of holes as a sieve," Lee retorted icily. "And your orders were that he was to be given maximum freedom."

"Compatible with security. I thought anticipation was one of your strong points."

"I've got four mobile men at my disposal," Lee said angrily. "With nine square miles to cover. And for all I know one of those four could be an enemy agent. Do you expect miracles?"

"It's not what I expect," the other replied with cold significance. And after a few moments of strained silence: "You have taken the necessary steps to prevent a repetition?"

Removing the headphones Lee rose from the chair and moved across to glower at the map.

"According to you he has made contact with an outside influence."

"The block precludes any other explanation."

"He must have made contact somewhere

in the hills. The Erdam will pick up through light foliage but not solid earth and rock, which means some kind of hollow. There are three such." His fingers stubbed at the map. "He has made two contacts already. There could be a third."

"I would consider that inevitable," the doctor agreed heavily. "If he is given the opportunity."

Lee smiled mirthlessly. "I intend to give it him. With all three places covered. According to the survey there is no alternative way into the valley. Which means his contact must be one of us. But aerial surveys aren't infallible. Someone could have found a way through the hills — perhaps in all innocence. If they did, then there's only the one place they could have come from. Blandon is only two miles away as the crow flies."

Crowther puckered his face thoughtfully. "Blandon?"

"Kinery SK-39," Lee told him. "With a staff of fifty-six. It could be one of them. I've asked Security to check if there's been any absenteeism during the past few days."

6

ALAN FELT NO SURPRISE at finding the doctor's car drawn up outside the house. The bonnet, he noted with a kind of grim humor, pointed in the right direction, away from Cradhill. Or from where Cradhill was supposed to lie. Lee, wearing a short-sleeved scarlet shirt, rested rawboned elbows along the top of his gate while he enjoyed a cigarette.

"The wanderer returns," he greeted Alan pleasantly. "An afternoon on the tiles. With the doctor cooling his heels in your parlor and demanding to know what had happened to his pet patient."

Alan leaned against his own gate while he hooked out a piece of gravel that had found its way into his shoe.

"I didn't intend to be away so long," he said steadily. "I found myself a spot out of the sun, lay down and I suppose, dozed off."

"Your return," observed Lee conversationally, "wasn't from your usual direction."

"A change is as good as a rest."

"Too true." The other showed his teeth in his usual sideways grin. "If I were you, old son, I'd go and pay my respects to old Crowther before he blows a fuse."

All very friendly, and all very ordinary. Neighbors exchanging badinage in the afternoon sun. And inside the house:

"Exercise," remarked Dr. Crowther, filling the hypodermic syringe, "is all very well. So long as you don't overdo things." The syringe spurted a jet of colorless fluid. "Are you ready?"

Alan was rolling up his sleeve. Whatever the purpose of the injection he couldn't refuse it. The needle stung. There was the usual brief moment of exhilaration. Rolling his sleeve back he asked: "What is that stuff?"

In the act of returning the syringe to its case the doctor paused for a moment. Then: "I thought you knew, Alan. It's an anticoagulant, to make sure you don't have a permanent blackout."

"I'm afraid I have to tell you, Doctor," Mrs. Low said primly from the door, "that we missed our afternoon tablets."

Crowther shook his head reproachfully. "We can't have that." His smile was a condescending creasing of solid fat. "We will forgive you this once. But it mustn't happen again."

When they had gone Alan went to stand by the window, automatically rubbing his arm and staring out at the garden. A charade . . . A stage set with a painted village and cardboard houses. The actors came from the wings, said their pieces and retired to await their next cue . . . A play written for one man.

Who was the author?

The sun, dipping now toward the hills, slanted a tree shadow across the window, turning part of it into a mirror.

Just for a moment his reflection blurred, seeming to waver and change, becoming a man with thick black hair and smiling, slanting eyes.

The silent voice was there too, whispering deep inside his mind.

"Match them at their own game," it said.

Now his own face was back again in the glass. His own face? The features were even more alien than that other — the slanting dark face.

I can't stay here, Alan thought. I've got to get away. There has to be a way out of the valley. . . . The way Karen came.

"And where would you go?" asked the silent voice.

"Your tea's ready, Mr. Fraser!" Mrs. Low called cheerfully from the kitchen.

Where do I start? he asked himself, leaning on the front gate, willing the second voice to be there to answer.

"At the beginning," it told him.

Monday morning. That was the beginning. The van had passed on its way to the village. It hadn't come back. There was only the one place to which it could have gone. That was something he'd worked out once before. But They had been there to make sure he didn't go through the farm gates.

"Try again," whispered the voice.

"Taking the evening air?" Sybil asked brightly, leaning over the adjoining gate.

"Too good to waste indoors," he told her, and stepped out into the lane.

"If you come across that wayward husband of mine," she called after him, "tell him I want to see him."

He heard the rattle and splutter of the green van some time before it came in sight. He stepped to the verge and waited for it to pull up as he had known it would. And yet, oddly, it was hardest of all to think of Fred in the same terms as the others. The others had fallen into a group. Fred Tolley seemed to stand a few paces away from them, a man apart. But he had to be one of them for all that.

"No rest for the wicked," Fred smiled, bare brown elbow jutting over the door. "Urgent delivery for old Tarvin."

"But a pleasant drive out into the country," Alan said.

"That's one way of looking at it." The other leaned out to inspect the view as if seeing it for the first time. "It is nice out here. And where are you off to?"

He had been expecting that question, but there was no satisfaction in the confirmation.

"Oh — as far as the top, then back again."

"To the old farm. It's a crying shame about that place — good land going begging." Fred's eyes twinkled. "You ever fancied yourself as a farmer, Mr. Fraser?"

Unaccountably, an excuse was being dropped in his lap. So where was the catch? Cowen had deliberately turned him away from the gates. Fred was offering him a reason to go through them.

"Farming," Alan said carefully. "Now that's an idea."

The other shielded his face in mock dismay. "Now what have I been and gone and started?"

"It might not be a bad idea to look the place over," Alan said. "When it was occupied, did you ever deliver goods there?"

"We're wholesale only. Shops, you know. Not private houses." The van started to move away. Fred held his hand up. "Be seeing you around, Mr. Fraser."

There was no sign of the Major, but Tony Verity was busy outside his cottage, scraping with a knife across a paint-encrusted palette.

"You could," Alan observed, looking at the multicolored oblong of wood, "frame that, just as it is, as an impressionist work."

Verity dipped the knife in a jar, partly filled with pink-stained liquid, that had been set on one of the gate-posts.

"A remark like that," he observed without rancor, "is calculated to strain even the closest of friendships. It suggests that my work is without rhyme or reason. All the same"— holding the daubed palette at arm's length —"there is a certain pattern to this, a certain cohesion of shape and color. Perhaps a touch of green here ——"

And bringing his knife-holding hand round in an elaborate sweep his elbow tipped the jar, knocking it off the post. Alan caught it before it touched the ground, miraculously without spilling any of the contents.

"Well held, sir!" cried Verity with surprise. "Deftly done indeed!"

"You're welcome," Alan said, returning the jar to its place.

The green van came chugging back as he rounded the next bend. Fred raised his hand but didn't stop. And behind came Lee, striding along without a care in the world, hands deep in his pockets of his slacks, calling while still some distance away: "You're walking overtime today, old son. Hillward bound again?"

"Only to the top of the lane," Alan replied without slowing his pace. "I've a message for you from Sybil. She wants to see you."

"Which means she wants the back lawn cut," Lee said, and turned about smartly and fell into step. "I'm in no mood for odd jobs this evening."

So there it was — escort duty, the whole thing accomplished simply and slickly. Two neighbors out for an evening stroll. Sybil had seen him go, Fred had picked up the trail, Verity had been ready waiting, Lee was the final link in the chain. And outside his shop, as they passed, George Tarvin just happened to be smoking an evening, shirt-sleeved pipe. They were leaving nothing to chance. It wasn't going to be easy getting away tomorrow afternoon to meet Karen again. But he would find a way. . . .

They came to the farm gates. Metal gleamed dully from the bottom rung. They both saw it together, but Alan was the one who stooped to pick the object up. There was an oddly familiar feel to the weight of it on his palm. Lee deftly appropriated it before he had a chance to examine it closely.

"What is it?" Alan asked.

The other was disinterested. "Search me, old son. I've no head for things mechanical." He slid the object into his pocket. "Most likely part of a car engine. Probably off that old van that Fred drives — it always looks like it's ready to fall apart. I'll give it to him next time I see him."

And then he consulted his watch and took Alan's arm in a firm but companionable grip.

"Getting on for suppertime, old son," he said. "Shall we wend our way back?"

The room was small and windowless with sterile white walls and ceiling. In one corner was a gray metal filing cabinet. A tubular chair with a round seat stood against a plain metal desk. Above the narrow door was a clock, the face divided into twenty-four segments. There was an overall smell of antiseptics. Dr. Crowther, his face expressionless, sat at the desk, leaning forward to inspect the object Lee had just laid there.

"An automatic pistol," Lee said. "A Beretta."

"Almost a museum piece," said Crowther,

who had never seen such a weapon before.

"Very nearly. But there are still a few in circulation. They're used by the E.S. boys. Lethal enough, and easily able to be slipped in the pocket. Each one has a serial number. Records are kept. This is the actual one issued to Hagan Arnold."

"So?" Crowther sat back, watching the other's face.

"Someone had carefully laid it on the bottom rung of the gate. Fortunately I was with Alan when he found it. I got it away from him and out of sight before he had a chance to inspect it closely. I told him it had dropped off Tolley's van. It would be just as well if you could confirm that at the next p.m. check."

The doctor touched the weapon with curious fingers.

"So it has to be someone who knew him well. An associate of some kind."

Lee nodded. "I had already assumed that. This is confirmation. And another move in the game, linking with the phone calls, not the attack. The attack was something very different. I'm almost certain we're dealing with two different people. And again, I'm practically certain one of them must be Gregory Gallea, whoever he may be."

"The C.P.C. people have no record of the name," Crowther said. "They've passed the query on to D.I.S. Which means the report will come directly to you."

"I was on to them earlier this evening. They didn't mention it then. They passed on the report from Kinery SK-39. The overseer who prepared it strikes me as being an over-zealous type. He might bear watching. His report was nothing if not voluminous."

Lee took a sheet of paper from his pocket.

"Two thousand and sixty head of cattle. Daily output of processed carbohydrate, two tons plus. Lactate products, one ton plus. Subsidiary bi-product's —"

"Spare me the details," Crowther said sourly.

Lee permitted himself a smile. "I thought you might be interested in life in a State Kinery. All right. Three columns of statistics. We'll forget those. Now — a staff of fifty-six. Absenteeism, nil. Very definite about that is our over-conscientious overseer. But three members on authorized leave."

"Have you got anything or not?" the other demanded testily.

"I've had D.I.S. check all three leave-members. We can forget two of them. The other — Karen Summer S34-46-15. Female manual worker grade 3. Age, twenty-four. We can forget the physical characteristics. She's served eighteen months in the Food Production Service, the last three in the State Kinery at Blandon. Prior to that — three years in the Hospital Service, two in —"

"Why this one?" Crowther broke in impatiently.

"I'm coming to that. She originated from a single allocation unit. Both parents now dead. Her last relative — her father's brother — died a year ago." Lee paused. "He lived in Beecher's End."

"So that's it." Crowther said in a flat voice.

"So it would seem." Lee folded the paper. "Her intrusion is probably innocent. According to the D.I.S. report she's in the clear. I'm having her brought in." He lifted one eyebrow inquiringly.

Crowther stroked his chin thoughtfully.

"If she is the one she may have spoken of it to others at the Kinery. That will be your concern. So far as I am concerned, the damage is unfortunate but not irreparable. Her presence has created a block that cannot be moved. Neutralization is only temporary. The p.m. will have to be extended, and she will have to be adjusted in terms of it. At one time in the Hospital Service?"

"A nurse."

"That should be the answer. It will mean a certain amount of delay, but that is unavoidable. Let me have her as soon as you've finished with her."

"You can have her in due course," Lee said, "with the compliments of Internal Security. Incidentally there is something else I think you ought to know about. I don't know whether it's of any significance."

"Let me be the judge," the doctor growled.

"I told you that Alan and I spotted the gun at the same time. I was nearest, but he got hold of it first. He moved like greased lightning without any apparent conscious effort. And Verity reported something similar. He was supposed to be cleaning his gear outside his cottage. There was a jar on the gatepost and he accidentally knocked it off. Alan caught it in midair. Verity said Alan was standing some distance away and he moved so fast the whole thing was a blur."

"What time was this?"— sharply.

"Oh"— Lee looked startled at the other's reaction —"about 21.00. That was when we found the gun. The episode with Verity must have been about thirty minutes earlier."

"Can you describe his actions more accurately? Were they intentional or automatic — reflex?"

"My job's security," Lee pointed out coldly. "If you want scientific data then you'll have to arrange for one of your people to take over surveillance."

"I thought your people were trained observers. When are you having the girl picked up?"

Lee glanced at the clock. "The green boys should be on the job about now."

"Good. And your plans for tomorrow?"

"If he follows his pattern, Alan won't try anything in the morning. I think he will try to slip away again in the afternoon." Lee smiled sourly. "Only this time his girl friend won't be waiting for him."

"But someone else might be," Crowther said heavily.

"Take care of your end of things. Leave the question of security to me."

Crowther's face set in a gray mask of hardness.

7

"KAREN SUMMER, SIR," Lee said formally, placing a thin sheaf of papers on the desk.

Crowther pushed aside the work he had been engaged upon, removed his spectacles with a tired gesture, pinched the broad bridge of his nose between finger and thumb and looked over his fingers at Karen. "Sit."

Karen, who had been on her feet during the earlier interrogation, sat down thankfully. Folding his arms, Lee leaned against the wall.

Crowther leafed through the papers. "According to this," he observed without looking up, "you have spoken to no one of your meetings with Alan Fraser. Why is that?"

"I haven't been at the Kinery long enough to make friends," she explained. "At least, none I can confide in."

"Which is very fortunate." He turned a page. "Three years in the Hospital Service —"

"Hospital SHG-68, sir. Nurse, grade 4."

He finished reading to the foot of the page, pushed the papers aside, removed his glasses again and holding them between large white fingers leaned forward to inspect her closely.

"Yes." He seemed satisfied with his inspection. "You have caused us a great deal of inconvenience. Fortunately for you, unintentionally. We were under the impression that the road is the only way into the valley. It seems we were wrong. You have met and talked with Alan Fraser. What is your opinion of him?"

"We only met twice, sir," Karen said evasively.

"That doesn't answer my question. All right, let me answer it for you. You met by chance, you talked, there were certain things that struck you as being odd."

"Yes, sir."

"You discovered that he believed he had been born and lived all his life in this village, which you knew to be impossible. You did discover that, of course?"

"At the second meeting, sir."

"And it was only natural that you would try to correct that impression by telling him it was impossible. How did he react?"

She hesitated. "I think he was ready to believe me. I had the feeling he would have to be on his own to work it out for himself."

"What else did you discuss?"

"He told me about the odd things that had been happening."

"Including certain telephone calls?"

"Yes, sir."

"Did he mention the names 'Hagan Arnold' and 'Gregory Gallea'?"

She had already been subjected to a similar interrogation, but a much more exhaustive one. "Yes, sir."

"A State-graded nurse," said the man behind the desk. "Which means you are an intelligent woman. Intelligent enough to know that something unusual is going on here. And also"— he paused for a moment —"intelligent enough to realize that you have been brought here for something more than questioning."

"I have been brought here to make sure I don't talk about the things Alan told me," Karen said in a dull voice.

"That, and something more. You will listen carefully to what I am about to tell you. You will not interrupt.

"Hagan Arnold was born thirty-six years ago in a small isolated village in Australia. His grandmother was Polynesian. From her he inherited facial characteristics that could pass as Oriental. He had a natural gift for languages. His parents died while he was still very young, and he was subsequently brought up by a Chinese family that had settled in the district before the movement restrictions were imposed. From them he learned the Cantonese dialect. At the age of fifteen he was drafted into the Australian Food Production Service. An overseer recognized the potentialities of his Eastern appearance and knowledge of the Chinese language. Arnold was transferred to one of the External Security Training Establishments, and in due course of time was posted here to England to complete his training."

Crowther paused. "You are familiar with the present world situation as a whole?"

"I read the news sheets," Karen told him. "I watch the authorized videocasts."

"A dutiful citizen of the State," he said dryly. "So you will have some knowledge of the situation existing between the Western Alliance and the Sinoasian Peoples Republic. Our Propaganda Service is very efficient, but they only issue that information which they think the people should know. In a well-ordered State there is no place for information that might cause alarm.

"You will know that the tension between East and West is of long duration. It developed into what has become known as the Psychowar some forty years ago when the West applied restrictions upon all frontier movement and the Tangs retaliated with even greater restrictions. They closed their frontiers completely, and the Bamboo Curtain came into being."

Lee spoke for the first time. "Tangs," he commented briefly. "You may not have heard the expression. It is used mainly in the Services. The Yellow Communists. The yellow-red people. Tangerines. Tangs."

"We are indebted to you," Crowther said coldly, and turned back to the girl. "Russia and her satellites, regarding themselves as neutrals, have taken no part in the struggle. Up until now — and for the sake of mankind as a whole we hope the situation persists — neither the West nor the Tangs have been prepared to risk open hostilities. With both sides possessing stockpiles of nuclear weapons neither would gain from warfare. The only possibility of the stalemate being broken would be if one side were to develop a completely new type of weapon and bring it into use before the other side realized its existence and found a defense. We in the West have to ensure that if the Tangs do develop such a weapon we have full knowledge of it right from the drawing-board stage. It is therefore vitally essential that we have agents working for us inside the Bamboo Curtain. There is a branch of External Security composed of carefully selected and trained men. Hagan Arnold was one of the finest of these.

"Unfortunately the Tangs' counter-espionage has been more than a match for the agents we have sent behind the Curtain. The incidence of capture and elimination is disturbingly high. With one exception, no one we have sent behind the Curtain has ever returned. But from time to time reports do filter out. And from those reports it is clear the Tangs are working on a new kind of weapon.

"A year ago Hagan Arnold, his training completed, was prepared for his mission. I use the word 'prepared' deliberately. It is essential that the agents we send out should not, under any circumstances, divulge information to their captors. A psycho-barrier is planted in their minds, triggered to take effect — completely obliterating all their memories — the moment a certain pain-level, either physical or mental is reached. I am one of those concerned in the placing of such barriers.

"Hagan Arnold was landed on the Sino-asian coast. For nine months there was silence, then a message came through. He had discovered something of vital importance, something too complicated to send in the usual way. He asked to be lifted out. A helijet was used to pick him up from an island and take him to Italy. But the plane crashed and exploded while landing. Arnold was the only one who came out alive. He was badly burned, and the pain had triggered the psycho-barrier into being. His memory had completely gone.

"After three months in hospital, where, among other things, he had been given a new face, he was brought to me. I was ordered by the Prime Director of State to break the psycho-barrier and extract the vital information locked away in his mind. I knew that it would be impossible to break that barrier using the same medico-mechanico-hypnotic system that had placed it there. I had to devise a method of persuading his subconscious to divulge the information without it realizing what was happening.

"And all this"— Crowther lifted his hands in a gesture —"is the outcome. An artificial man in an artificial life. I set the raw material of mind and body in a mold of my own design. We call that mold the psycho-matrix; p.m. for convenience. There had to be no connecting links between his old life and the new. A new past, a new present, a new place, even a new time.

"Alan Fraser, living in Bewdey — names chosen at random. The p.m. obviously lacked the smaller details. So to it was added the knowledge that from childhood he had been subjected to blackouts. This would explain to his mind any gaps in his past. A motoring accident explained the scars of the facial grafts. He was told that he was a writer, and it was strongly impressed he must write to earn money. His thoughts, from the first moment of waking to his new life, were guided toward the subject of a novel he had to write. A selection of names was offered for the choice of his main character. It was essential his subconscious believed that choice to be free. His selection of the right name — his own name — told us that the experiment stood an excellent chance of succeeding. We hoped that for his novel he would write what actually happened to him behind the Bamboo Curtain."

Crowther leaned back. "Have you understood all that?"

"Yes, sir," Karen said.

"Certain incidents have occurred that threaten the structure of the matrix. Some of these you will already know of. We are coping with them satisfactorily. But there are others that indicate the presence of an outsider — other than yourself — in the valley. Mr. Craig, my chief security officer, will explain them to you. The p.m. will have to be adjusted to accommodate your presence. While that is being done quarters will be found for you here at H.Q."

He paused again, regarding her closely. "If you are as intelligent as I think, you will have guessed the real reason why you were brought here."

"Yes," Karen said with an effort.

"Your presence is not part of the matrix. We cannot afford the time to remove you from his mind. We may not even be able to do that. There is only the one answer — both you and the matrix must be adjusted. You will be doing the State a great service. You have no objections, of course." It was a bald statement, not a question.

"I have no choice, sir," she replied.

"You have a choice of a kind," he corrected. "You can either undertake the work voluntarily, or else —" He left the rest unspoken.

"Or else you would have to condition my mind," she finished for him.

"I'm afraid so. But that would waste a considerable amount of valuable time."

"And my service in the Kinery?"

He waved that aside as being a detail beneath his consideration.

"Mr. Craig will arrange the formalities of your temporary attachment to Internal Security. You will be used as a nurse, of course. A uniform —" He looked at Lee who nodded curtly.

"I'll take care of the details."

"Good." The doctor raised one hand in a

gesture of dismissal. "That is all for now, Nurse."

She followed Lee outside. In the white-walled, harsh-lighted passage he smiled at her for the first time since they had met.

He frowned along the passage. "Now where shall we bed you down for the rest of the night? Tolley's on radio duty. You can have his room."

He led her along the plastic-floored passage. At the end he stopped, considering for a moment and then taking her arm to guide her to the left.

"I'll put you in the security picture while I have the opportunity," he said, and pressed a button in the wall. The lights flicked out and a door hissed aside to reveal the night valley. Karen stepped into the open, drawing in air that was sweet after the stale flatness of the past two hours. The ghost of a drive, overgrown with weeds, led toward a gate. Beyond, the road snaked away, a moonlit ribbon between dark trees and hedges.

"This is the old farm," she discovered.

"It was." Lee leaned against the side of the doorway behind her, taking out his cigarettes and offering the packet past her shoulder. "Genuine Virginian. One facet of the p.m. that benefits us all." He cupped his hands carefully round the glow of his lighter.

Karen drew in the smoke gratefully, and was conscious of a relaxing of a body made taut by tiredness and apprehension. What Crowther had told her had come as no great surprise. She had already decided, had been ready to tell Alan, that something of this kind must be the reason for the creation of his artificial existence.

She was oddly relieved that his loss of memory had been caused artificially and not intentionally. Now she was to meet and become one of the people he had told her about. She hadn't made up her mind about Lee Craig yet. So far she had seen two sides of his character and she wasn't particularly enamored of either. But she understood both — the cold inquisitor, and she had had dealings with D.I.S. men before — and the man making a pass, and those she had met and dealt with before.

Turning, she held up the cigarette.

"Alan's cigarettes were one of the first things that puzzled me. I didn't like to ask him outright how he came by them."

"Imported," Lee said briefly, "along with certain other commodities that fit into the p.m. background. But I didn't bring you out here to discuss trivialities. I want to make your position clear to you to avoid any misunderstandings. Professor Amos Crowther of the Department of Counter Psycho-Conflict is nominally in charge of operation Newlife, but only by virtue of seniority. I am responsible for all security and you will come directly under my jurisdiction."

"Yes," Karen said without turning.

"He will tell you the precise part you are to play in the p.m. Other than that you will take orders from me and from no one else."

The moon hung low, a fat, buttery globe

that almost tipped the somber shapes of the hills. Somewhere in the shadows was a house where a man lay sleeping. And for that lonely man, all this. . . .

"Very good," Karen said.

"When you get out there you will have to be on your guard all the time. It isn't very easy. I'll have Sybil talk to you." He carefully stubbed out his cigarette. "Alan has told you about the phone calls. They were obviously an attempt to undermine the p.m. There is something else. An attempt was made to kill him."

She turned then, one hand to her mouth, aghast. "Kill?"

"It almost succeeded. I am working on the assumption that, unlikely though it seems, there are two Tang agents among us, working independently of each other.

"My department is taking the necessary measures to try to locate them. In the meanwhile, everyone must be regarded as suspect. I want you to keep your eyes and ears open and report to me anything unusual that occurs, no matter how trivial it may seem. The personnel here will be told of the circumstances behind your joining Newlife. They will know you come under duress. There is always the possibility that one of the agents may see in you a possible ally. If you are so approached, no matter how deviously, you will fall in with any suggestions made, and then you will report to me. Is that clear?"

"Yes," Karen said in a small voice.

"Do you know how to use Erdam equipment? I believe some of the Psycho Hospitals are furnished with it."

"Erdam?" She shook her head. "I've never heard of it."

"Extended Range Directional and Amplifying Microphone. That is a gap in your education I'd better fill at the first opportunity. It might come in useful."

He moved to her side.

"I think that's all. Except that I cannot impress upon you strongly enough the vital importance of the success of the operation. It could mean the salvation of the Western Alliance. Have you any questions?"

She had just one.

"What will happen to him — Alan — when all this is over?"

"What will happen to him?" That it was clearly something he'd never thought about was answer enough in itself. He shrugged. "That isn't for me to decide." He moved back into the passage and Karen followed to stand at his side.

"The next time you cross this threshold," he told her, reaching for the button, "you will be stepping back fifty years into the past. Which is quite a thought." He showed his teeth in a smile.

She stared at him. "Into the past? I don't understand."

"Crowther wasn't very clear on that point," Lee said. The door hissed back into place and the passage filled with glaring brilliance. "A new past, a new present, even a new time. Remember? A new time. Even that had to be different to obviate any connecting link between his real and artificial lives. You have to learn to forget that this is the Year of the State, 2016. Out there in the valley it is the Year of Our Lord, 1966."

Some time later Dr. Crowther made his way wearily along the passage that led to the rear of the converted farmhouse. He stopped at the murmur of voices from the radio room, opened the door and went inside.

Fred Tolley, shirt-sleeved and tieless, leaned back from the control panel to remark: "You look all in."

Propped against the bench, Lee said: "I was just coming to see if you were still up. A preliminary report on Gregory Gallea's just come in. He's a D.E.S. man and was actually one of Arnold's contacts in Sinoasia. So far as they know he's still mingling with the Tangs, but they're checking to make sure. The trouble with the D.E.S. crowd, they can move about to their hearts' content without having to render an account to the State. So he could be back in this country."

Crowther palmed red-rimmed eyes. "He could have defected."

"Always a possibility. Incidentally, Arnold was carrying that Beretta at the time of the crash. Which could be a useful lead. They're looking into it. Another thing I wanted to talk to you about; when are you bringing Alan in for the p.m. adjustment?"

Crowther uncovered his eyes.

"It will have to be done as soon as possible. And in such a way as not to disturb the present matrix. The first opportunity will be when he takes his morning tablets. I intend replacing the usual depressant with a boost analeptic sufficiently strong to induce a blackout."

"I would rather you left it till later in the day," Lee said.

"The adjustment will take at least six hours. If I leave it till evening, another day will have been wasted." Crowther's eyes narrowed warily. "What do you have in mind?"

"If he is left alone he may try to slip away again in the afternoon."

"He will certainly try to do that."

"So I want him to do just that."

"No," Crowther said firmly. "I had been half-expecting that. You want him as bait for a trap. No."

"I will probably never have such another controlled opportunity. If it does bring one of the Tangs out into the open, if another attack is made on him, I can promise he will come to no harm."

"The risk is too great. No."

"It would appear," Lee said coldly, "that you have little faith in the security measures placed by the State at your disposal. I would remind you that you aren't the only one acting directly upon the Prime Director's personal instructions. I wouldn't like to put in my report that an attempt by Security to apprehend an enemy agent had been prevented by the medical staff."

"You have already failed to prevent one attack."

"Which was unexpected. The next one won't be."

"I protest!" Crowther cried angrily.

"Your protest will be duly recorded," Lee rejoined blandly. "So that is agreed then. You will not commence treatment until evening."

Crowther swung savagely on his heel to wrench the door open.

"One more thing," Lee called after him, and the doctor stopped in the doorway. "What significance, if any, do you attach to the speeding-up of Alan's reflexes?"

"I fail to see," the other fumed, "how that can be any of your concern."

"His safety is my responsibility. Any change in his behavior is important."

"I see." The doctor sounded disgruntled. "It is nothing you need to take into account. The apparent speeding-up of his reflexes is merely a side effect of the temporary imbalance between the analeptics and depressants with which he is being treated. Once the dosages have been adjusted the effects will disappear."

He slammed the door behind him.

"One up to our side," Fred commented softly. "Analeptics, sham-aleptics. You think he knows what he's talking about?"

"Huh?" Lee turned from a pensive contemplation of the door. "Yes, I'll give him that. According to the Prime Director he's the State's leading authority in his field."

"And the great Julius Minsterly is never wrong." Fred rested his elbows on the metal bench and yawned hugely.

Lee said: "Nothing else is likely to come in tonight. If it does, the web-recorder can take care of it. Turn in and get some sleep. I want you up again at first light."

"Okay." Fred obediently fed a webspool into the auto-recorder and adjusted a dial. "All set. What have you in mind for me?"

"The laser-gun used in the attack. I've had all the buildings checked. It's not the sort of thing easily hidden."

"I know what they look like," Fred said dryly.

"It's got to be kept dry." Lee tugged at his ear. "But that doesn't help much. I think — I'm sure — that it's wrapped up in something — plasto-sheeting, possibly — and stashed somewhere in the hills, probably not far from where the attack was made."

"Great Julius!" Fred exclaimed in dismay. "Two miles of bushes. What's the chance of getting hold of a vibro-detector?"

"No time. You'll have to do it the hard way. Start with the slopes at the back of the house."

Fred turned a third yawn into a grin. "I suppose I click for the job because I was in the clear at the time of the attack."

"When I give you an order," Lee said bleakly, "there doesn't have to be a reason."

8

THE LASER-GUN was a metal tube some two feet long, a handgrip partway along its length, that tapered toward the blackened nozzle end. The bulky power-pack and activating mechanism container at the other end was curved to fit against the shoulder, but the green-uniformed Internal Security Police, to whose sole use the weapon was strictly confined, preferred to operate it from waist height, where the beam of concentrated, searing light could be employed to encompass a wider swath of destruction.

On his hands and knees in the bracken, Gregory Gallea carefully wrapped the gun in the black plasto-sheet before placing it deep inside a gorse bush. Squatting back on his heels he looked carefully about him and then rose to his feet to climb the few yards back to the path. He looked ruefully at the damp patches on his knees. The heavy dew that jewelled each frond, each blade of the wiry grass, would vanish as the sun climbed higher. At the moment it was still touching the hills, sprawling his shadow ahead as he walked quickly back toward the village. There was no stir of breeze. The air was langorous and heavy. There was a sullen bank of clouds outlining the hills in front. Gallea thought that perhaps a change was coming in the weather.

Stretching, yawning, Alan inspected the morning from his window. No hill mist this morning. The sky overhead was still high and clear, but behind the hills was an ominous piling of thunder-gray clouds. By the electric feel of the air, the look of those clouds, a storm might be on the way.

The smells of coffee and frying bacon were the usual background to shaving. But to them, at least for a few moments, so that he paused with razor poised, was added something new. The bathroom was above the kitchen and there was a tiled floor between, but he could hear Lee's voice quite clearly, and Mrs. Low answering, and interspersed with their desultory conversation the distinct and identifiable sounds of a drawer being opened, cutlery clattering, a plate being set on the metal top of the cooker, even the hiss and splutter of bacon in the pan.

The sounds faded, leaving only the muted whirr of the shaver, and he finished stroking the night's growth of bristle from his face without any sense of wonder, as if the temporary increase in the acuity and range of his hearing had been a perfectly normal thing.

Back in the bedroom he selected clothes for the day. Something lighter than even yesterday. A silk shirt, no tie, certainly no jacket. His face and neck, he discovered, were no longer painful. He went downstairs.

"All very casual." Lee, cup in hand, leaning as usual against the open back door, eyed the shirt. "Elegant and devil-may-care into the bargain." But he too was wearing only a shirt, one of some light cellular material. There were fine lines etched at the corners of his eyes, Alan noticed without having to stare, and the eyes themselves looked drawn and heavy as if their owner hadn't slept too well.

"We're in for a storm, I shouldn't wonder," observed Mrs. Low, bringing plate from oven to table in one deft movement. "Thunder, even."

There was a short silence.

"Did you escape having to mow your lawn?" Alan asked, making conversation, knowing that like them he was only acting a part in a charade, feeling not at all disconcerted by the unnaturalness of it all, but supremely confident in his ability to match them at their own game.

"Upon my return I was tired to the point of exhaustion," Lee grinned. "I sank wearily into a chair and was ministered to by a wife who had forgotten all about foot-high grass. So I suffered a temporary welcome reprieve. And how's the book coming along, old son?"

"Quite well." Oddly enough he had known that question was going to be asked, even had the answer waiting on his lips before the words were uttered.

And the next one too. That he answered: "I hope to make real headway with the rough

draft of the remaining chapters today,"
while Lee was still asking: "And what had
you in mind for today?"

Then Lee was silent for a few minutes,
not looking at anything in particular, not
frowning, just letting his eyes slip around
the room.

Mrs. Low left to start work. Lee said, with
what seemed an effort: "Well, I'll leave you
to get on with the good work," set down his
empty cup and wandered away.

Alan enjoyed his breakfast. The food, he
fancied, had more flavor about it than anything he had ever eaten before. It took a
certain amount of experiment to determine
the exact amount of sugar required to adjust
the coffee to his precise liking.

In the study, seated at the typewriter,
words thronging in his mind, jostling to be
set down on paper, he still paused, leaning
back and lighting a cigarette. He knew, because it was the obvious thing, that the reason behind his artificial existence was the
writing of the novel. But not the book itself;
a rough draft apparently would satisfy them.
Not a literary masterpiece, just a sequence
of certain events. They wanted the story of
Hagan Arnold's experiences in Sinoasia. And
they wanted it quickly. So it had to be important. Hagan Arnold, as Karen had first
suggested, had to be a real person. If it
wasn't for the fact the narrative was to be
set fifty years in the future — Lee's sugges-
tion, that — he would have felt certain that
it was his own story he had to tell, and that

114

he himself was Hagan Arnold. Or had been, before he had changed into the feeble apology for a man who was Alan Fraser. But Alan Fraser wasn't so feeble now. Alan Fraser wasn't Alan Fraser any longer. He had become Hagan Arnold again. How that could be, with fifty years to be accounted for, he didn't know. But he felt certain that he was Hagan Arnold. He puzzled about that fifty years' difference. For a moment the answer seemed in the forefront of his mind. Then it went again. That was something he intended discussing with Karen when they met that afternoon. He wondered, as he bent over the typewriter, what she was doing.

She was sitting on the side of a small metal bed in a windowless room with white walls and the minimum of furniture. On the glass-topped dressing table against one wall was a man's hairbrush and shaving tackle. She tried to picture Fred Tolley whose room this was. He was one of Them, but Alan had referred to him as his "particular friend." Which in a way was strange, because Lee, his confidant and neighbor in the play, should have qualified for that distinction. She had the feeling that They intended Lee to fill that role. Tolley, who by all accounts only came into the village at certain intervals, should have occupied very much a background position.

Earlier, Lee had brought her breakfast on a tray, told her that it would be tomorrow before her services would be needed, pointed

115

out the bathroom, and ordered her, once her
toilet was completed, to stay in the room
until told she could leave. The key turning in
the outside lock had given more than the
impression of being in prison. The place had
fallen silent and the time dragged. She found
an unusual gap when her watch told her it
was ten o'clock, the time for the first of the
State news videocasts, viewing of which was
compulsory, and there was no stereoscreen
to be switched on and no unsmiling news-
caster to read out information from his
three-dimensional tank.

Hands clasped behind her neck she lay
sideways across the bed staring up at the
sterile ceiling. The sound of heavy footsteps
brought her upright. The door opened, and
the brown-faced, grizzle-browed man who
entered seemed to fill the room. She gazed at
a uniform that she had seen before, but only
in pictures.

He removed the clumsy, uncomfortable-
looking helmet and placed it on the bed at
her side before seating himself with a sigh of
relief on the only chair the room boasted.

"Cowen." When he smiled there was a
deepening of the already deep lines from
nose to corner of mouth. "Albert Cowen.
Constable." He reached for the tight collar
of his uniform. "You'll have to get used to
the sight of this fancydress." He nodded
toward the discarded helmet. "Julius knows
how they managed to wear them without
getting a perpetual headache." There was a
red score across his forehead that had to be

116

massaged with rueful fingers. "And the appliance they have given me to ride has to be seen to be believed." His smile became friendly, even fatherly.

"Craig asked me to look in on you to see if you were all right." She knew what that meant — to make sure she was still safe in the room. But why the check when the door was locked? "And to start the process," he finished, "of putting you in the picture. I take it that so far you have only met Crowther and Craig?"

Karen nodded. "But Alan told me quite a lot about the others."

"That's something. And you've got twenty-four hours to find your feet. They won't be bringing him to the lab before this evening. How do you feel about your enforced assignment?"

"I am content to be able to serve the State," she said woodenly, knowing that that was the answer she was expected to give.

Cowen was silent, watching her and tapping the mat of gray bristles on his upper lip with a contemplative finger.

"Mr. Craig told me that I wouldn't be needed till tomorrow," she ventured when the silence threatened to become strained. "Professor Crowther —"

"Doctor Crowther," he broke in, correcting sharply.

"Doctor Crowther. I'm sorry. He gave the impression that every second counted. Why is he waiting till this evening before bringing Alan in?"

"As a member of the State Security Forces," Cowen said, "the first thing you have to learn — which you should have learned already — is to obey instructions without questioning them. That applies to all the Security personnel here. I can't speak for Crowther's own staff. Let me give you the general picture. Peter Clamp, George Tarvin and Mrs. Low . . ." He paused, one eyebrow raised questioningly.

She nodded. "Alan did mention them."

"They are Crowther's own people. The rest of us are all Security. We have all been triple-screened by D.I.S. Whoever was responsible for the attack on his life — you know about that?"

"They told me."

"Whoever it was, couldn't have been a member of Security — for all a laser-gun was used."

"A laser-gun?" Her pupils dilated. "I didn't know that." Then: "The circle of new cement on the wall —"

"A near miss," Cowen said evenly. "If Alan hadn't passed out when he did he would now be minus a head. And until we discover who was responsible — and for the phone calls as well — his life will remain in constant danger."

At eleven o'clock Mrs. Low brought in the morning tablets. Alan took them in his palm, neatly covered them with his thumb as he lifted his hand to his mouth, swallowed and sipped water. When she had left the room he slipped the tablets into his pocket. Then he returned to his desk. Eight pages of typescript lay face down by the typewriter. He had written them without having to think, and they represented Hagan Arnold's first few weeks behind the Bamboo Curtain. He flicked through the pages, reading rapidly. So far as he could tell nothing of significance was mentioned. Neither had Gregory Gallea come into the narrative. It was odd about that name, so familiar, and yet with no mental picture to match the familiarity. Until a picture did form, Gallea would have to remain in the shadows.

There was the sound of the van chugging along the road outside and he glanced automatically at his watch. Fred was much later than usual this morning. When the ragged engine sound, instead of passing by, faltered and stopped, he came to his feet and went into the front room to look carefully from behind the curtains.

Lee, cigarette dangling nonchalantly from lips, hands in the pockets of his slacks, lounged against the side of the van, grinning and chatting to Fred in the most natural manner imaginable. The window was closed, the road was some distance away, but Alan could hear the murmur of the voices although not the actual words. By a sudden burst of mutual laughter they were enjoying a joke together.

"I expected to have heard from you before now," Lee laughed. He was a man who never took chances. There was always the possibility that Alan might have heard the van arrive and had been drawn to the window. "Did you have any success?"

Fred played his part in the mock hilarity.

"It was up there all right. I tried the rock face beyond the knoll first, figuring that a dry crevice might be a likelier place than a bush in the open. I found the place where it had been stashed — small piece of plastosheet and disturbed stones. Then I went along the path. It took me three hours to find it. Tucked in a gorse bush, wrapped in plasto, and the sheet was bone dry. Heavy dew last night, the sun hadn't got to it, so —"

"So it must have been switched from crevice to bush earlier this morning," Lee finished for him.

"Which is all very significant and nasty," Fred said, laughing.

"Did you interfere with it at all?"

"No. I was of two minds whether or not to remove the power-pack, but you hadn't given instructions, so I left it as it was."

"Good," Lee replied approvingly. "Take the van to the village in the usual way, then drive it back and park it. Then make your way back to H.Q. I'll be in touch later. If you want to contact me, don't use the phone."

Fred leaned forward to throw the clutch. He put up his hand as the van moved away. Smiling, whistling cheerfully, Lee walked back to his house.

After lunch Alan went upstairs to lie

120

down. That was expected of him. It wouldn't be clever to change any part of his routine unnecessarily. They must already have their suspicions. There was no point in giving them further grounds. This was a cat and mouse game, but with the odds still very much on the side of the cat.

From his bedroom now, through closed doors, he was able to hear and identify the sounds of Mrs. Low in the kitchen. This time he did wonder a little at this new increased sensitivity of hearing. So far as he could tell it wasn't there all the time, only when he needed it. A voluntary, rather than an involuntary ability. Like now, when he had to know just when Mrs. Low was ready to finish, so that he could go down to the study and be ready to slip away the moment she went upstairs.

He had managed to evade them twice already. Now they would be on their guard. He was one against — against how many? — three: Mrs. Low, Lee, and Sybil. And perhaps some of the others would be waiting to intercept outside. The cat and mouse game, and he was enjoying it.

A clatter was Mrs. Low replacing the top of the stove. Alan came to his feet and went swiftly and silently down to the study. The first move in the game, and just at that moment he was finding more pleasure in anticipating the battle of wits ahead than in the purpose behind the operation, the meeting with Karen.

When Mrs. Low, her routine remaining

undisturbed, he wondered a little about that
— had gone upstairs he went through the
kitchen to stand in the open doorway while
he looked out at the garden. The air was even
heavier now than it had been first thing. Not
a branch, not a blade of grass stirred. Any
alien movement could be instantly detect-
able. He glanced briefly at the sky. Clouds
still lowered menacingly purple above the
hills, but overhead was still clear. The threatened storm should hold off until evening. He
went quickly across the lawn and into the
bushes. And still nothing else moved. He
could hear Mrs. Low in her bedroom, singing while she changed. Now he was through
the hedge with the hazard of open ground
before the next shelter of the copse.

There was the sudden impression of eyes
watching every move he made. He listened
intently, accepting unquestioningly the message of his new, awakening senses. Nothing
moved but the feeling persisted, intensifying
as he ran toward the trees. There he stopped
again, listening, not panting, not even
breathing heavily after the sudden unusual
exertion. His ears caught the faint snap that
could have been made by an incautious foot
coming down on a piece of dried twig. His
senses alert, the blood singing in his veins,
he moved silently along the green-arched
glade, knowing with certainty now that he
wasn't alone. With only a little effort he could
reach his mind out and gather in the
thoughts, the impressions of the other person. With a little concentration. . .

He had stopped, frozen into a statue, before the whistle and thud of sound. The haft of a knife quivered in the trunk of a tree inches away from his face. He stared at it, puzzled, wondering why the alien thoughts he had picked up a moment before had held no message of threat. His mind reached out again and this time found nothing. Whoever had thrown the weapon had gone. He grasped the haft. It required an effort — so thrown by an expert, his instinct told him — to free the blade. Then he balanced it on his palm, six inches of gleaming steel and a plain wooden haft. But not entirely plain, for there was a streak of blue paint down one side, and he recognized it, remembering that the last time he had seen it had been outside Tony Verity's cottage when it was being used to scrape paint from a palette.

Lee had selected a hollow where he had the backs of the houses and one side of the copse in view. Over to the left, hidden by the copse and a rise in the ground, was area C.19, fifty square yards of heather, bracken, and gorse. In one of those bushes, so Tolley had reported, the laser-gun was hidden. The attack, when it came, he felt, would be launched from somewhere in that area. Whoever the enemy agent might be he wouldn't risk carrying the bulky weapon for any distance in broad daylight. Changing it from the crevice to the bushes in the first light of day had been a different affair. He assessed the lie of the land. The trap was as efficient

as he could possibly make it. Tolley, the
only one of his men he could even begin to
trust, should already have taken up his position overlooking the area from higher ground.

He used his binoculars to scan Alan's
house. A dimly-seen shape moving in the
window was Mrs. Low in the kitchen. Lee
brought down the glasses while he glanced
at his watch. Zero hour, if Alan followed
the same plan as the two previous times,
should be in ten minutes. Mrs. Low had been
instructed to adhere to her normal, rigid
timetable.

He relaxed, turning on his side, and a jab-
bing pain reminded him of the Beretta he
had slipped into his pocket. He took it out,
weighing it on his palm. This was the first
time he had had occasion to examine such
an antiquated weapon since leaving the D.I.S.
Training Establishment fifteen years ago.
There were six shells in the magazine. He
worked the breech mechanism a few times,
satisfying himself that it was in good order.
Then he slid it back into his pocket and
picked up the glasses again. Mrs. Low was
still in the kitchen. He wished that he could
have afforded to take the risk of using at
least one other of his men. But he could easily have picked on the enemy agent himself.
Tolley, in the clear at the time of the first
attack, was the only one he dare use.

When he used the glasses again they
showed him an empty window. He swung
them the fraction to cover the door, focusing

124

on it just as Alan emerged. The speed with which he covered the exposed garden was startling enough, even at that distance, to cause Lee to draw his breath sharply. This was something he hadn't taken into account. Only a temporary thing, so Crowther had assured him, that unnatural speed of movement.

He watched Alan break cover and race toward the copse. Now you see him; now you don't. Swearing savagely under his breath, Lee swung the glasses over his shoulder and came to his feet, crouching, moving as swiftly as the ground would permit, circling the copse so as to be ready and waiting at the other side.

Fortunately it took Alan longer than he had anticipated to negotiate the stretch of trees. When he did emerge Lee was waiting, gun now in hand, to follow the path some distance above, his eyes scanning the bushes ahead and below. This was area C.19. This was the trap. And the man below, the bait.

The feeling of invisible watching eyes was back again, stronger than before. Alan slowed his pace, his eyes alert, forcing his mind to reach out ahead. It brought back a strange confusion of impressions. There was hatred, and apprehension, and watchfulness, and strangely enough, a fleeting sense of anxiety and concern.

He sensed the movement in the bushes some distance above the path and had

125

stopped, turned, and was half-crouching, ready to meet the man who came plunging down the slope toward him, even before that man had risen to his feet.

In the same moment that he recognized Fred Tolley's stocky form, before he even had a chance to register surprise, his mind shrieked warning of danger, swinging him round on the impulse-axis of speeded-up reflexes to meet a threat from a new direction. He sensed the brilliance that lanced from a clump of bushes some distance ahead before the light sprang into being.

Tolley reached the path in a flurry of rubble, his mouth a black circle, mouthing words that were lost in the alarm clangor in Alan's mind. He flung himself instinctively at Tolley in an effort to hurl him from the path, and they went down together, struggling, rolling over, while the ground where they had stood an instant before burst into searing white-hot flame. Pain lanced along his side, there was a moment of flaring agony and then the black mercy of oblivion.

9

"ONE NURSE'S UNIFORM," Lee said curtly, tossing a bundle on the bed. "*Circa* late twentieth century, or as near to it as they could get at such short notice. It should pass muster. Put it on and then hold yourself in readiness."

"How bad is he?" Karen asked through tight lips.

"You'll find out in due course," he told her and went out, locking the door behind him. Thunder growled distantly as he went along the passage. As it died away the sound was taken up by the hum of generators and the insistent pulsating of equipment in the treatment room at the far end of the passage. The door of Crowther's room was partly open and he stopped to look inside. The doctor was writing at his desk. Lee went inside, closing the door behind him.

"I need something for my report," he said.

The doctor removed his spectacles with a gesture of tired resignation.

"Yes. Your report. The burn covers a wide area but is fortunately only superficial. There is no danger from it. Do you need more than that?"

"I think so," Lee said.

"The affected area has been successfully covered with synthoflesh. He has received three seroplasmic transfusions. At the present moment he is in the first stage of mechanico-subthalamic hypnosis. That is all I can tell you." He leaned back. "I was just preparing my version of the incident."

"I thought perhaps you were," Lee said dryly. "I would like to make it clear that I can accept no responsibility for what happened. And in my own report I intend to point out that you are entirely to blame for the failure of the plan."

"And how," Crowther asked tonelessly, "do you arrive at that interesting conclusion?"

"The scheme worked out precisely as I had planned. Tolley had taken up a position overlooking area C.19, from where I anticipated the attack being launched, as indeed it was. I was in Alan's rear. Tolley detected the actual ambush site just as Alan came in sight. He immediately moved down to cut off the assailant's retreat, but Alan intercepted and attacked him. During the resultant confusion the enemy made his escape."

"Confusion," the other echoed significantly.

"Caused solely by Alan's unpredictability. I was relying upon your earlier statement that his unnatural speed of movement was a temporary thing and would disappear under adjusted treatment."

Crowther thought for a moment before

opening a drawer and taking two tablets from it. He laid them on the desk.

"I accept a certain responsibility," he said, choosing his words carefully. "These are the tablets I intended he should take this morning, and which would have rectified his behavior. They were found in his pocket when he was undressed. Mrs. Low has been reprimanded."

Lee said: "I will note your comments in my report."

"I would rather you didn't," the other said evenly.

"Understandable," Lee admitted coldly. "But an official report must always be complete in every detail."

"Which is precisely what I was telling myself when you came in." Crowther laid a third object alongside the two tablets. "I was persuading myself it was my duty to report this."

Lee looked at the knife. "Where did this come from?"

"It was also removed from Alan's pocket. It has been identified as the property of one of your men. Anthony Verity. There were no prints on it."

"Verity."

"I am sure your superiors would be most interested to hear an explanation of how a lethal weapon belonging to one of your men found its way into Alan's possession."

Lee's face set in a granite mask.

"Have you spoken to anyone else about this?"

"Only to Mrs. Low who found and identified the weapon." Crowther creased his face
in a colorless smile. "If Verity does happen
to be our fly in the ointment I am quite certain you would rather discover that fact by
any other means than one that smacks of
gross inefficiency."

"It would seem," Lee said, cautiously de-
fensive, "that both the medical and security
staffs have been guilty of inefficiency."

"I would much rather my work was allowed to continue without outside interference," Crowther said smoothly. "Any mention of apparently unnatural behavior on the
part of Alan might attract such interference.
It would be repugnant to me, as I am sure it
would be to you, to have to submit to State
supervision."

"There is still a report to be written," Lee
said.

Crowther spread his hands. "The trap you
laid for the enemy was excellent. It failed
only because Alan suffered a blackout —
which is the truth so far as it goes — before
the trap was sprung." He pushed the knife
across the desk. "What you do with this is
entirely your own affair."

Lee hesitated before picking it up. Then
he laughed.

"Stalemate," he said with reluctant ad-
miration. "This time, at least. You scratch
my back, I'll scratch yours."

Doctor Crowther wasn't amused. Neither
did he display any signs of triumph. "I prefer to regard the present position as a step

toward a better understanding." He picked up his glasses. "Perhaps you would be good enough to ask Nurse Summer to report to me."

Karen found the antiquated nurse's uniform to be both ugly and uncomfortable. It was the first time she had worn a skirt and the loose sweep of the fabric against her thighs made her feel naked and unnatural. There were no stockings — women had worn such articles of clothing at one time, she recalled from her school days — and she was thankful for their absence. It took her a few minutes, once she had donned the blue dress, to master the complications of stiff white apron with loose bib, and the impracticable strip of white fabric intended for use as head-wear. The shoes were of the old-fashioned type, not unlike those Alan had worn — and she had puzzled a little about those at the time — with the further complications of short lengths of black cord to be threaded through eyelets.

Lee escorted her along the passage without passing any comment upon her appearance, simply saying briefly that Doctor Crowther was ready to give her her instructions. He left her when they reached the door.

The doctor leaned back from his work, removing his reading glasses and inspecting her closely.

"Yes. I think that the bonnet — if that is the correct term — should be set farther back on the head." His eyes traveled downward. "They provided no stockings?"

"No, sir," Karen said, adjusting her hair.

"A pity. If he happens to remark upon their absence — let me see. You have lost one pair; the others are at the laundry."

"The laundry?"

He smiled. "In its way the forerunner of the State Clothing Recovery and Issue Service." He came to his feet. "I think the time has come for you to meet your patient, Nurse."

He held the door open for her with an old-fashioned courtesy that she found strange. They went along the passage. At the door at the far end he stopped.

"Have you had any experience with mechanico-medico-hypnosis techniques, Nurse?"

"None at all, sir. I served in a General Treatment Hospital."

"Post-operative care of synthoflesh treatment?"

She nodded to that. "Yes, sir."

"Excellent. But please remember that from now on you must address me as 'Doctor' and not as 'sir.' All right?" His smile was geniality itself. "Your patient will be under depth-hypnosis for some time yet. When the matrix adjustment is completed he will be removed to the room next door. It will then become a ward in the Cradhill General Hospital. You will be present when he wakes. He will recognize you, which is inevitable, but not as the woman he met on the hills.

You will be the nurse who took care of him after his accident ten years ago. He will remain in the ward at all times until I issue orders to the contrary. No one is to visit him without my permission. He must not be left unguarded under any circumstances. That is vitally important. You will find a bell-push inside the door. When you do have occasion to leave the ward you will press the bell and then wait outside until someone comes. I have arranged for Peter Clamp to be available for that duty.

"The date will be June 17, a Friday. The year, 1966. You will find those details entered on the temperature charts at the foot of the bed. Did you have any occasion to study Comparative History while at school?"

"I didn't specialize"— she remembered in time —"Doctor."

"But you will have a fairly general knowledge of the late twentieth century?"

"Yes, Doctor."

"Craig will help you fill in the details." He fingered the flabbiness under his chin. "I think that is all for the time being."

Taking a key from his pocket he unlocked and opened the door.

The banks of equipment that surrounded the solitary bed were all strange to her. Alan, wearing only a pair of white shorts, lay motionless on the top of the bed, his eyes closed, his arms straight at his sides. His left side, from armpit to waist, was swathed in the fluid bag that she recognized immediately as the postoperative treatment of applied syn-thoflesh. Narrow strips of gray plastotape were fixed across his bare chest, his wrists and ankles.

"A normal precaution," Crowther explained smoothly, watching the direction of her eyes. "There have been isolated occasions when a sudden outside noise has disturbed the coma and given rise to a temporary convulsion."

Karen followed him to the side of the bed. A metal band held six contact-points in place across Alan's forehead. Wires trailed from each to one of the pieces of apparatus. Padded earphones were clamped to each side of his head, connected with the equipment set on a metal table at the head of the bed. It was from that equipment that the insistent, monotonous thudding came, pulsing in time to the pendulum needle that clicked steadily, almost hypnotically, across a triangular dial.

"No doubt you will find it all very confusing," Crowther said.

She started impulsively to reply: "I find it all —" and then broke off, barely failing to repress a shudder.

"I can assure you that it looks more complicated and alarming than in fact it is. The patient is now in the ultimate sub-degree of depth hypnosis, a state which very few scientists have been able to achieve. The addition to his present psycho-matrix has been verbally recorded on webspool, reduced to thalamic impulses and is now being played back to him. It is as simple as that.

134

"That" — indicating the soft-clicking metronome needle — "is the control stabilizer that maintains the hypnotic rhythm during the implantation process."

He glanced up at the clock set high in the wall immediately beneath one of the unshielded glaring lights.

"Each hour he receives an injection of Palagistrone, a preparation of my own devising, composed mainly"— he smiled fleetingly —"if you still remember any materia medica, of an alkaloid extracted from the root of a plant called rauwolfia serpentina. It is a subthalamic stabilizer. Unfortunately it also acts as a depressant. When the patient wakes he will still continue to receive regular injections of Palagistrone but to counteract the depressant effect it will be necessary for him to receive carefully graded dosages of a booster analeptic. It will be one of your responsibilities to ensure he takes the tablets I shall provide you with, at the times I shall specify."

The insistent click and sweep of the pendulum beat time to the thud and pulse of the apparatus. The musty dry smell of electricity mingled with the tang of some antiseptic. The man on the bed was a waxen image, with only the slow rise and fall of his chest to show he was alive.

Crowther looked approvingly round the room and then took hold of Karen's arm.

"A unique experience for you, Nurse," he observed, and now the former pedantic pomposity had become replaced by undisguised pride. "And one which few people have the privilege of sharing. I can say without hesitation that this is the latest and by far the most efficient of the psycho-matrix-induction techniques that have so far been evolved."

Outside in the passage, with the insistent throbbing beat pursuing, seeming to vibrate the very air itself, he turned from carefully locking the door.

"And now," he told her, "you had better return to your quarters until such time as you are sent for."

Back in the cheerless room Karen sat on the side of the bed and stared at the wall, setting on its sterile emptiness the picture of a pathetic waxen dummy, surrounded by and attached to the hideous incomprehensible trappings of an unholy science that was adding even more unreality to an already completely artificial and unnatural existence.

And after a while, trembling uncontrollably, now, she rested her face in her hands while the waves of shuddering became a flood of bitter, hopeless tears. She never realized that in her anguish she had called a name aloud.

Alan opened his eyes.

A glaring brilliance that made him wince; brightness that was harshly painful to the point of physical impact. The muted, steady pounding of cotton-wool drumbeats deep inside his head.

He could turn his head with an effort, but that was all. There was a stiffness down one side, and his arms and legs were immovable. He twisted his head to one side, looking backward and upward. A pendulum swung easily, its sweeps synchronizing with the drumbeats in his mind. He stared, concentrating on the moving sliver of steel. It faltered, recovered, completed its sweep and then stopped, quivering. And with it stopped the hypnotic beating.

And now the discomfort of the lights.

Caution, his mind warned. His eyes traced the wiring to the switch on the wall by a door he could just see by raising his head. The switch moved, clicking softly, and the room was plunged into a blackness sprinkled with dancing stars.

He experimented with his right arm. The plastotape bit into flesh, but gave, so that he could tell that increased pressure would cause it to break.

Careful, his mind warned again, and he relaxed.

Now he let his mind have its way, feeling it reach out seeking the source of the voice that had brought him awake. His thoughts were a tenuous tentacle, feeling their way through swirling mists. They found, and immediately identified, a cloud of alien impressions. His own name was there, in the soft cadences of a woman's voice, and sorrow and pity and tenderness. And hatred too, but for someone else. And fear, of what was happening. And again, that wailing sorrow and compassion . . .

He mouthed *"Karen"* soundlessly, and set

his thoughts traveling again. Another cloud, this time farther away, no larger than the palm of his imagined hand, dwarfed, made almost incomprehensible by distance. This time a man's thoughts, unidentifiable. Trivial impressions. The mind of someone relaxing and letting his mind drift. Food . . . real butter, real bacon, real coffee, real cigarettes. . . Alan frowned with the effort of concentrating, finally finding a name. So Peter Clamp had left his little post office and was here. . . .

Where was "here"?

His mind could sense but not see. There were no windows to this room. Only shapes seen dimly against a darkness that had become smoothly velvet with the passing of the aftermath of the glaring brilliance.

His new faculty, untrained, almost as yet untested, would not be capable of journeying any great distance. There had been a place where Karen wept, another that held Peter Clamp. And there was this room here. So it had to be a fairly large building. If he was still in the valley, and he felt sure that that must be the case, then there was only the one building it could be. Alan smiled in the darkness. He had found his way into the farm after all.

Tired after his efforts he closed his eyes, letting his head fall back. But the warning voice roused him. *"Don't sleep,"* it told him.

He wasn't ready, yet. He was only just on the threshold of learning the way of the new being that was himself. As yet he had only toyed with some of the powers at its disposal. And until he was ready, They must not suspect anything. When They came back They must find the light on and the pendulum moving. That was why he must stay awake, to turn a switch and set a sliver of steel in motion.

There was one thing he could do, or try to do, while he was waiting. He sent his thoughts out again, this time deliberately seeking that first cloud that had been made up of a woman's tears and compassion and hatred. He found it after a while, but now it was faint, barely perceptible. And he sent a message along the waves of his thoughts.

Karen, he thought, *don't worry. Everything will be all right. . . .*

And Karen, weary after the storm of weeping, lying back on the bed, closing her eyes, willing sleep to come, sat up with a jerk, her eyes wide, searching the room, finding nothing, but hearing Alan's voice as clearly as if he were standing there at her side.

But he wasn't there, it was impossible that he could be, and so the voice could only have been in her mind. She must have fallen asleep and then awakened to the echo of a voice from an already forgotten dream. And yet — so vivid. She lay back on the pillow again. Some magic in the dream-voice was feeling its way through the tangle of worries and fears in her mind, smoothing, soothing, relaxing. . . . Closing her eyes she was asleep almost instantly.

She awoke to a feeling of confidence and well-being. Her watch told her it was one o'clock, but whether it was early morning or afternoon she had no way of telling. Coming to her feet she smoothed down the skirt to which she was already becoming accustomed. The door was still unlocked and she went along the passage to the bathroom. The water was tepid but refreshing.

The place was silent and deserted. Strangely silent, for as she went diffidently toward the door at the end of the passage no sound of pendulum beats came from behind it. She tried the handle, but it was still locked. Puzzled, she retraced her steps, pausing at the door of Crowther's room, tapping softly and then opening it, finding nothing but blackness inside. She continued along the passage, turning the corner, passing her own room, coming finally to the thicker door that guarded the far end of the light-filled passage. She found the wall switch that flicked out the lights and then set the door hissing back into the wall.

The air outside in the open was sweet and fresh after the antiseptic smell of passages. There was no moon — perhaps it was covered by the heavy cloud banks that piled above the hills — hills so close she could have reached out to touch them — but the faint starlight picked out the shape of a path and, as her eyes became accustomed to the darkness, the darker silhouettes of a cluster of farm buildings. Or what still seemed from the outside to be farm buildings. For all she knew, the barn, with its high-sloping roof, could be a shell housing another white-walled, windowless laboratory. And the stables might well contain a powerhouse, or the van that Fred Tolley drove — the van that had been another of the things she had found puzzling when Alan had mentioned it, for with very few exceptions all goods' vehicles on the roads were of a standard type, all bearing the markings of the State Transport Service and all driven by gray-uniformed State drivers.

In the pocket of her uniform was the carton of synthatine tubes — all that was left of last month's allocation — which she had transferred from her corduroys when she had changed. She placed one of the thin tubes between her lips, inhaling sharply to ignite the tip, drawing in the smoke and finding it tasteless after the smooth satisfying flavor of Alan's Virginian cigarettes.

Relishing her moments of pseudo-freedom, wondering only in a desultory fashion what would happen if one of Craig's security men were to find her out-of-doors, she walked slowly along the path and then turned off it while still some way from the outhouses to wade through tall grass toward the darker shadows of the trees.

It was strange, she mused to the stars, how a voice in a dream could sound so lifelike and have such a reassuring effect. Before, she had been worried and frightened, shocked to the point of hysteria by what she had seen happening to Alan. Knowing what must have been done to him, and actually seeing it being done were two very different things. That was when her hatred for Crowther and the science he represented had been born.

And now — if she closed her eyes she could still hear Alan's voice — how did she feel about the artificial man now?

She was still worried and afraid for him, but not to the panic-degree of before. Her hatred for Crowther had subsided into a kind of cold acceptance of his powers.

And for herself? She drew on the tube and then stubbed it out in a small shower of sparks. She had no feelings for herself. She had been brought into the world by the State Maternity Service, educated by the State, drafted by them into a State Factory, transferred to a State Hospital, transferred again to a State Kinery. And now the State had transferred her yet again. She belonged to the State. Her thoughts were those the State had trained her to think.

And yet. . .

The small seed of rebellion? But that was unthinkable.

Atavistic defection, they called it, and must be corrected. Defection from the ideals of a State-controlled twenty-first century to the dark-age, uncivilized, uncoordinated ideas of the Elizabethans of the twentieth century. And for such defection, not uncommon, the State Department of Correction, Psycho-Correction. A mystery — but not such a mystery now after what she had seen — behind high walls and barred doors.

So rebellion, even the hint of it — unthinkable.

And yet . . .

Out of the darkness behind her two hands came, one to clamp her arms tightly to her sides, the other to press, stifling, over her mouth, so that fighting was futile, shouting impossible.

A voice, a man's voice, whispered urgently in her ear.

"Don't struggle. I'm not going to hurt you. I'll take my hand away if you promise not to make a sound. Nod. . . ."

She nodded. The hands were withdrawn. Not frightened — she was sure she wasn't frightened, her pulse raced only from being startled — she turned to face the man. He had stepped back into the shadows. Just an ordinary man, no uniform as far as she could tell. Just an ordinary face, what little she could see of it — only gleaming eyes and white-shining teeth — and one she was sure she hadn't seen before.

"I only want to talk to you," he said. "I need your help. My name is Gallea. Gregory Gallea."

10

HE STOOD in the shadows, not very tall, his dark face almost on the same level as hers.

"I'm sorry about that," Gallea apologized, smiling, "I can assure you that wasn't my normal way of approaching a lady. But I couldn't risk you making any sound. Would you have screamed?"

His voice was friendly, calm, and very matter-of-fact. He was giving her chance to recover from being startled, Karen thought. And perhaps at the same time trying to inspire confidence.

She matched his tone. "I may have done. That sort of thing's never happened to me before."

"I've been watching you for some time. I had to be sure you weren't followed. You were smoking a synthatine." He held out his hand. "You'd better let me have the rest of them. If Craig caught you smoking one of those on duty he'd flay you alive. And we don't want anything like that to happen to you."

Obediently she placed the slim package in his hand. He had another to offer in its place.

"Take these. The gen-u-ine thing." He

made two words of it. "Better than that synthetic muck in any case. I know the creed is land for food and not tobacco leaf, but it doesn't help make them taste any better. If anyone asks how you came by them you can always say Alan gave them to you." He showed his teeth in another smile. "I hope that's put our new relationship on a firmer basis."

"Who are you?" Karen asked steadily.

"I told you. Gregory Gallea. If you mean, what am I, then I'm certainly not an enemy agent." He shrugged. "But I can't expect you to take my word for it just like that. Not after the indoctrination Craig is sure to have given you."

"You said you needed my help."

"So I do. The first time in my chequered career that I've had to turn to a female for aid and assistance. I find the experience sobering. I want you to help me get Alan away from here."

"Where to?" Shocked, it was the first thing she thought of.

"Julius knows! I haven't reached that far ahead. A question of first things first. But I'll think of somewhere."

"Are you one of Mr. Craig's men?"

He seemed content to let her ask questions, answering with a lightness of tone and a frankness that could be deceptive.

"For my sins. And at my own request. I volunteered for the job. You'll be introduced to me formally in due course, in my part as one of the occupants of this salubrious and nonexistent village. I only hope that when the time comes you won't point the finger of betrayal in my direction and shriek 'enemy agent' at the top of your voice."

"I'm not shrieking now," Karen said.

"So I'd noticed. But perhaps you consider conditions unfavorable for such a demonstration." He spread his hands. "I'm unarmed. I'm also of a gentle nature. And despite an extended diet of real instead of synthetic food I haven't developed any animal instincts. The cards are stacked your way. I'm putting my life in your hands, talking to you like this. That should be guarantee enough for my good intentions. All I want you to do is listen to me and decide if you can agree to help."

He lost his smile. His voice became serious.

"If you don't agree, you will be doing Alan incalculable harm. And not only him. . . ." He paused. "They'll have told you the reason behind all this?"

"The village?" She nodded. "They told me everything."

"I'll warrant they didn't," he retorted grimly. "They will have told you just enough to be a rational explanation and to make you feel it was your bounden duty as a good citizen to give all the help you could."

He paused again, stepping to one side and looking toward the house.

"Do you know who's in there now?"

"I didn't see anyone when I came out."

He smiled a little. "That figures."

"Dr. Crowther and Mr. Craig were there

earlier." Why was she talking to him so freely? "I didn't see anyone else. Apart from Alan."

"So they let you see him."

"Yes," Karen said in a small voice.

"And did you like what you saw?"

She was silent to that.

"Out here," Gallea told her, "you can talk. They haven't got round to dubleming the trees yet."

"Dubleming?"

"There speaks the voice of innocence. You'll learn as you go along. Our Internal Security people have a passion for planting microphones. Small fellows, little larger than the head of a nail. Micro-mikes. Double-Ms. Known as dublems in the trade. They fixed them in every room of every building in the valley the moment they knew something was going wrong. You know about the phone calls I made?"

"Alan told me about them himself."

"I'd like to know what his reactions were. But that will have to wait. I can't risk being out here too long. I want to spend what time there is in trying to convince you of my good intentions."

He lifted one hand to his face to press thumb and second finger to the outer corners of his eyes in a gesture that held both weariness and indecision.

"So now I've got to talk fast and convincingly. And I haven't had time to sort things out. So where do I start? With Alan himself. Hagan Arnold. They'll have told you some-

147

thing about him, but not what kind of a person he was. And that's important. We worked together for a long time, and yet I never once saw his face. The one time that I did see him he was — unrecognizable.

"The last thing he wanted was to be forcibly drafted into External Security. And yet he became one of the finest agents they had ever had. But he was like that with everything he did. A brilliant mind, a horror of killing, and a detestation of regimentation. An individualist, and Julius knows, there aren't many of that breed these days. In the eyes of the State individualism is tantamount to out-and-out defection. The odd thing about it was although he never went out of his way to make a secret of his opinions, they let him get away with them. And that's damned unusual.

"He was sent here from Australia to complete his training. I was going through the mill at the same time. They train agents in pairs, but they never see each other. Hagan was at a center somewhere up North. I was in the South. When the time came one of us would be sent inside Sinoasia, the other would stay somewhere on the fringes to act as outside contact. Training in part consisted of the sending of pseudo reports, the idea being that we would get into the habit of communicating with each other. There's no time to go into details, but between us we evolved a fake code, once we had discovered we could trust each other and that our ideas ran pretty much along the same lines. You

148

can learn a lot about a man, that way, in four years.

"Another odd thing happened during that time. For some reason, which even he himself was at a loss to account for, he was taken from the training center and dumped for two years in a State university. In one of his messages to me he told me he was happier than he had ever been before.

"When the two years were up he was returned to the training center. A few months later he was sent to Sicily, one of the jumping-off grounds for agents bound for the East. I followed a week later. He had already left by submarine. I was sent to an island off the Sinoasian mainland to act as his outside contact.

"For a long time there was no word from him. Then came the message saying he had stumbled on something important and wanted lifting out. I made the arrangements and was waiting in Italy for his helijet to arrive. They'll have told you what happened then. A damned stupid slip-up on the part of the pilot. The rotor blade hit a hillside and the whole thing went up in flames. I was the one who dragged what was left of Hagan from the flames. I won't go into details. When they had taken him away I collected his few possessions — those that were intact. I kept his gun, one of the old-fashioned automatics. He was put in an Italian hospital until his burns healed. They said he would have to be sent back to England for skin-grafts. . . ."

Gallea paused.

"They must have told you about the mind-blocks planted in the minds of every agent sent behind the Curtain. . . ."

"Yes," Karen said.

"Which meant his past had gone as well as his face. And with the past, the information he was supposed to have. . . . A group of C.P.C. boffins flew out to look him over. I didn't like the way things were going when they took over from External Security instead of merely cooperating with them as you might have expected. Like Hagan, I've never had a great liking for Crowther's Counter Psycho-Conflict mob. It was obvious they had something else in mind other than giving him a new face.

"So far as authority was concerned, I was still somewhere out East. I let them go on thinking that. I wangled a passage on the same jet that brought Hagan and the C.P.C. men back to England. Then it was a matter of changing my name, altering my documents — and I felt a certain amount of pleasure in using the methods taught me by the State, to fox the State — and getting myself downgraded, which was easy enough, from External to Internal Security. Being an ex-Grade E type I was allowed a certain amount of freedom and I was also in the position of being able to pull strings. When I got wind that Crowther himself was concerned with an operation called Newlife, with another big noise, Lee Craig, to be in charge of security, and when they both took to hanging about the hospital where Hagan was recovering from his synthoflesh grafts, I knew this was it. I had myself transferred to the operation. We came down here a fortnight ago. And I found out at the briefing what they had done to him."

Gallea paused again.

"This is where I've got to make you see things my way, not theirs. They say that the reason for all this complicated set-up is to force his subconscious mind to cough up the information. But that isn't enough. There's got to be something else. There's got to be another, more important reason."

"Mr. Craig told me that the information could mean the salvation of the Western Alliance," Karen said.

"But how does he know that?" he demanded, leaning forward intently, staring into her face. "They only have Hagan's word for that. All right, so he's one of their best agents. But is his word enough to bring the Prime Director himself down from his ivory tower to personally superintend the setting-up of the operation? Is it enough to bring Professor Amos Crowther, the most advanced of our scientists, away from his research to play the part of a twentieth-century G.P. out here in the wilds for Julius knows how long? Is it enough to bring Lee Craig, acknowledged to be one of the mainstays of Internal Security, away from his department to fritter time and talents away guarding one solitary man?"

He broke off, breathing heavily.

"I don't know," Karen said weakly, helpless under the deluge of demands.

"But I do. I know how their minds work. I've been trained for that sort of thing. They would only go to all this trouble if they thought it was something that concerned themselves personally. Themselves — the happy little racket of State regimentation they have built up — not the Western Alliance as Craig would have us all believe."

There was a short silence broken only by the rustle as Gallea changed his position. When he spoke again his voice was low and intense.

"I am almost certain I know what they are doing. Obtaining the information is only the excuse. Hagan was an individualist, a defector, and they knew that. But Correction would have meant the loss of one of their best agents. And more, it would have made a martyr of him. Perhaps sending him to the university was their idea of trying to persuade him to their way of thinking. You know the sort of thing — look, we are giving you this opportunity of bettering yourself. We can't be so bad, after all. . . . But it didn't work. In one of his last coded messages to me Hagan said that he regarded himself as an agent of the Western Alliance as a whole, not the slave of a totalitarian state.

"And then one day he is presented to them on a plate. The empty shell of a man who had been one of their greatest potential enemies. His past is still intact, but locked away in his subconscious. They can leave him as he is — as they leave all the unfortunates who undergo total amnesiac adjustment in the Correction Establishments — to work out a new future as best he can, with no past at all to build it on. Or they can try something new — for here they have the raw material of an acid test. They can try to give him an artificial past and present to guide his new future. They can turn him into anything they like.

"And if we can do it with this one particular man, they say, we can do it with anyone. And to make the test more stringent, more conclusive, we will give him an artificial past so completely different in every respect from his real one, that his acceptance of it will be proof positive of the experiment's success."

Gallea laid his hand on Karen's arm.

"Can you understand all that?"

She was silent for a moment before nodding. "I think so. . . .

Then: "You said, if they can do it to Alan, they can do it to anyone. But why should they want to do it? And what good would it be?"

"I'd've thought you could figure that out for yourself," Gallea said almost roughly. "Given time, you would. The State is still virtually in its infancy. It's still precarious. Time and energy and money have to be spent on keeping the population well to heel. How much easier it would be, how much more satisfying for Crowther and Craig and the rest of them, if the people were utterly and completely subservient, if they accepted and obeyed orders unquestioningly without the constant supervision of the State."

Understanding came to Karen on a shuddering tide of cold horror. Gallea rammed the thing home into her stunned silence so there should be no doubt at all about his meaning.

"People with no minds of their own," he said harshly, almost brutally. "Belonging completely to the State. A race of slaves."

"No," she whispered, refusing to accept the horror.

"I've done what I could to interfere with their plan," he said, his voice normal again, speaking steadily and calmly, giving her time to adjust her thoughts. "The telephone calls, mentioning his real name and mine. . . . I left his gun where he could find it. Did they tell you about that?" He went on without waiting for a reply. "It was the only way I could try to upset the psycho-matrix. That's what they call the thing they've done to him. I knew I couldn't make him remember his real past, but I could make him doubt the present. At least, I hoped it would delay things. I haven't tried to harm him. You should have realized that by now. I had nothing at all to do with the attempts to kill him. You've got to believe that."

Here was something her mind could grasp. Something solid. Something that was a relief from the crowding thoughts. And Craig himself had told her that two different people were trying to interfere with Alan.

154

"Two different patterns," she said. "Do you know who the other one is?"

It took him a moment to grasp her meaning. "The attempts to kill him. No, I don't. That does have to be the work of a Tang agent. After that first attempt I told myself it would have been better if it had succeeded. That's how I felt for a time. Anything rather than the success of the experiment. But when I'd had time to think . . . Hagan was my friend. And they'd got started, and if they lost one guinea pig they'd only find themselves another. I didn't see why Hagan should lose his life in the process. That's when I started figuring out ways of getting him away. But I didn't see how it could be done. There's no road into the valley at all. . ."

"There was a road," Karen said.

"There isn't now. They took away two miles of it, where it joins the main road, and they filled in with brambles and rubble. I thought about that. I could have tried to find a way out. But I didn't know how strong Hagan was — I knew they were keeping him under drugs — and I didn't know if they had anyone at the other end. Then I thought of trying to hijack the heli. It comes in most nights bringing supplies. But they'd have known something was wrong almost right away. We wouldn't have stood an earthly. Then you came over the hills. They didn't know there was a way through. . . ."

"It's a very rough path," Karen said. "About three miles, mostly climbing. It comes out at the Kinery. They have guards there all the time."

"It's the only hope," Gallea said.

"I don't know," she said helplessly. "I can't even think. . . ." She shook her head. "I can't believe all this."

He spoke calmly again. "No more could I at first. And I have to be honest with you. There are still some things that don't make sense to me. This set-up here . . . You'll find out for yourself. You'll be living way back in 1966. It's correct down to the damned smallest detail. The food, the clothing, the cigarettes, the way we talk, the furniture, even the soap and toothpaste. Everything.

"Hagan wasn't even born fifty years ago. He will have read about those times, seen pictures. You know, like everyone else. History. The Dark Ages of the Second Elizabethans, the State calls it. He called it the Golden Age. But at the best he could only have a general idea of what it must actually have been like. So you'd think a general background would suffice. But it doesn't. Every damn thing has to be correct down to the most minute detail. Which doesn't make sense. Maybe he's a perfectionist. Crowther, I mean. But I don't know.

"What I do know, what I'm sure about, is that my explanation for what is going on is the right one. And when they've proved to their entire satisfaction that a man of more intelligence than average — and a trained agent at that — can accept that he is living fifty years in the past, and be content to go on living there without querying it in any way, then the experiment will be judged a success. And if I know anything about them, once they're satisfied they'll wipe 1966 and everything about it from his mind and start all over again. Only this time the new past they'll put into his mind will be the one that will lead to a future completely subservient to the State."

"I still can't believe they'd try to do things like that," Karen said dully.

"Think about it." He rested one hand confidingly on her shoulder. "Think about it, but don't take too long. They've got to start all over again with Hagan, which will give me a few more days' grace, but there's still someone trying to kill him."

He took his hand away. "You'd better go now. You've been out here too long already. We'll talk again. And don't recognize me when next we meet. You know?" He showed his teeth in a smile devoid of humor.

"I know," Karen told him, and turned to go back to the house.

The door hissed into place, the lights came blazing on as she flicked the switch. The passage was empty. In her present mood she would not have cared if someone had been there, demanding to know where she had been, whom she had been with.

Back in her room — it seemed an age since she had left it — she sat on the bed and stared into emptiness. When she tried to think calmly about the things Gallea had told her she found it so impossible that when

157

she opened her mind it was flooded, over-whelmed by the unimaginably horrifying picture conjured up.

Men couldn't do those things to another of their own kind. They couldn't play with the human mind like a child with a slate. Wipe the slate clean of yesterday's picture, draw a fresh one there, wipe it away when its usefulness is done, draw yet another. . . . And the reasons for those pictures . . . . Men and women with artificial pasts on which to build artificial futures to the order of the State. Slaves of the State, Gallea had called them.

He had to be mistaken. Or else he was lying, trying to shock her into helping him. He wanted to take Alan away from here. That might be true, but he might also be an enemy agent.

What name did he use for his part in the charade? He hadn't told her and she had had too many other things to think about to ask him.

Not Lee Craig. Not Mr. Cowen. Those she had already met.

Not Major Holt. A retired officer would have to be an elderly man. Gallea looked to be in his thirties.

He had told her he was one of Craig's Internal Security men, but she couldn't accept that. That could be another lie. But it had to be one of four; George Tarvin, Fred Tolley, Anthony Verity, or Peter Clamp.

Her mind finding some relief in a problem

it could at least understand and try to cope with, Karen leaned back against the pillow.

According to Gallea, if he could be believed, he had never met Hagan — or Alan as she found it easier to think of him — but they had become friends. It could be that Alan still retained some sort of instinct that might enable him to unwittingly select one of the characters on the stage of his artificial life and label him "friend." It wasn't much to go on, but it was something. She closed her eyes. After a while she fell asleep.

She was aroused by the sound of a tray being set on the chair. The man who had brought it, dark-faced, elderly, unsmiling, she had not seen before.

"You are to report to Dr. Crowther as soon as you've finished," was all he said, closing the door behind him again as he went out.

Her watch told her it was eight o'clock. What little sleep she had managed to snatch had refreshed her. On the tray was a cup of coffee — real coffee, something she had only tasted once before and that was when she was a child — toast, buttered toast, real butter — another rarity, and a dish of some orange-colored confection that was completely strange to her. She tasted it delicately, savoring the sour-sweet tang, nibbling the small shreds of some kind of fruit peel.

Crowther's voice called "Come," to her tap on his door. Shirtsleeved, tieless, stethoscope dangling from his neck, he sat at his desk.

Lee was at his elbow, and both men looked up from the papers they had been examining. The doctor removed his spectacles.

"Ah. Nurse Summer. You slept well?" Just a polite inquiry, no significance in his tone.

"Thank you, Doctor."

Lee was silent, contenting himself with a curt nod.

"The patient has been transferred to the ward," Crowther said genially. "He will sleep for perhaps another hour. He will want to know why he is in hospital. You will tell him that he received injuries when a blackout caused him to fall sideways into a fire."

He produced a small bottle from one of the drawers.

"You will give him two of these tablets as soon as he wakes. Another two at eleven o'clock. That is very important." He glanced inquiringly sideways. "Craig?"

"Right," Lee said briskly, coming from round the desk. "I'll take over." He opened the door for her. "I'll fill you in while we have time. Cowen you've met already. Anthony Verity you can forget about for the time being. The man who brought your breakfast was Peter Clamp."

"I see," Karen said.

"Mrs. Low is at the house. You'll meet her later." He tugged at his nose. "And my loving pseudo-wife, Sybil." He led her along the passage and round the corner. An elderly man, almost bald and with an over-florid complexion sat cross-legged and bored alongside a closed door.

"The ward," Lee explained shortly. "And Major Robert Holt, our battle-scarred warrior."

Holt nodded without smiling.

They returned along the passage.

"Radio room," her guide said, stopping at another door. "Out of bonds at all times. Is that understood?" He opened the door wide enough for them to see inside without actually entering.

"Fred Tolley," Lee said of the man who sat in front of one of the equipment-cluttered benches. "When he's not operating our communication system he drives a van and delivers groceries."

Another man, with a dark face and frizzy black hair, leaned against a second bench.

"George Tarvin," said Lee. "Runs the village stores."

Tarvin had a greeting of sorts for her. "Our new recruit. Welcome to the fold."

Fred Tolley swiveled on his chair so that he could look at her and smile. She returned the smile.

"Alan mentioned you to me," she told him. "He called you his particular friend."

"That's nice," Tolley said easily. "We get on together all right. But then I make friends easily. Maybe we'll get to be as friendly."

"I'm sure we will," Karen told Gregory Gallea.

11

ALAN OPENED HIS EYES.

Still a white ceiling overhead. Still the
smell of antiseptic, but now no musty, dry
tang of electricity, no pulsating of machinery. The last thing he remembered was sens-
ing Crowther's return, and then reaching
his mind out to set the pendulum sweeping
and to bring the lights blazing back. He had
closed his eyes as the door opened. He must
have fallen asleep.

This was a different room. His arms and
legs were free. He experimented with his
mind but it had lost its previous clarity and
mobility. It felt sluggish, resisting his efforts to project. When he moved his arms
someone came to stand at his side. A blue
dress, white apron, strip of white fabric
across dark curls. His vision cleared but his
mind seethed against resistance.

"How do you feel?" Karen asked, smiling.

"I'm all right." With her help he pushed
himself into a sitting position. A small room,
windowless, sparsely furnished, a sink in one
corner. He was in a narrow, metal-railed
bed.

She had two tablets on a slip of paper. He
took them from her automatically, holding

162

them in his hand while he fought the mists. They started to clear. "Water . . ."

While she was filling a glass at the sink he transferred the tablets to the other hand. He kept them there while he made pretense of swallowing. His thoughts reached out at last, piercing her mind, finding confusion there, thought overlaying thought, a tumult of emotions, names, faces.

Handing back the empty glass made him aware of a tenseness in his side. His exploring fingers discovered tenderness.

"What happened?" he asked, and knew the answer before she told him. It sprang to the forefront of her mind along with other thoughts. She had been instructed to tell him he had burned himself as the result of a blackout. She didn't want to tell him that, because it wasn't the truth. But Crowther had given her orders, and obeying them was the only thing she could do until — until . . . The thought trailed away into nothing.

The tentacle of his mind probed in search of it, but found instead a name, two names. Gregory Gallea and Fred Tolley. Another strand linked them into one. He tucked the information away. Gradually his mind strengthened, but still there were mists and sluggish resistance. He found fear and anxiety amongst the tumult of Karen's thoughts and he wanted to tell her, as he had before, not to worry, that he understood what was happening, that he could read her mind. . . .

And deep in his own mind a warning shrilled, forbidding. . . .

He knew that Karen could be trusted. He knew from her thoughts that she was for him and against the others.

The others . . . Crowther and Craig and the rest of them. . . . Trained observers, trained never to miss a trick. A slip of the tongue, even a change of expression . . . Karen would be putty in their hands. She would never betray his confidence voluntarily. But if they were to use their devilments on her . . .

"Where am I?" he asked, because that was a question he would be expected to ask, and in their turn they would ask her how he had behaved, and they would know whether or not she was telling them the truth.

"You're in hospital, at Cradhill," she told him.

This is one of the rooms in the farm, her mind told him, but he knew that much already.

"I've seen you somewhere before." Her mind was waiting for that. It had the answer ready, the answer she had been told to give.

"Now fancy you remembering that! That was ages ago. You were recovering from a motor accident."

And so it went on. He had to play his part in the fatuous exchange of words. He found it detestable — almost degrading — but he was playing the part for her sake as well as his own.

He was thankful for the interruption of a distant mutter of sound.

"Thunder," Karen said, and her mind told him that she too was grateful for an excuse to bring the thing to an end. "A storm's been hanging about for some time now." She stepped back from smoothing the sheets and tucking them in. "That should be more comfortable. Now we must see about taking your temperature."

"The wheels of Odin's chariot," Fred Tolley remarked, glancing up at the ceiling as the distant rumble died away. "Or is it Thor? I've forgotten what little mythology I learned. Sounds like we're in for a stinker."

Tarvin was cleaning his nails with a small screwdriver. He didn't look up. "It may pass over," he said.

Tolley looked at his watch. "You had your grub yet?"

Tarvin nodded and belched.

Tolley grinned. "A sign of good breeding in Tang-land. Or used to be in the olden days. You can't rake up a belch on a handful of husked rice. You like to take over while I eat?"

Still scraping his nails the other slid absently into the vacated seat.

"Fifteen minutes," Tolley said from the door. "Nothing's likely to come through."

But he was wrong. The recoprinter clicked and hummed into life before the sound of his footsteps had died away. Not particularly interested Tarvin leaned sideways to watch the lines of print as they appeared. It wasn't until the message was complete and he had ripped it loose, had reread it and had time to think about it that he came to realize its full import. Then, his dark, almost Negroid, face set in grim lines he came quickly to his feet and made toward the door. And there indecision overcame him and he stopped, one hand reaching up to pluck his lower lip while a thoughtful expression replaced the previous grimness. He was still thinking when the other returned some ten minutes later.

"When this little lot is over," Tolley observed with mild regret as he came into the room, "and I have to go back to oleopaste, sawdust bread, and compressed meat substitute, I shall probably curl up and die of malnutrition."

And then he saw the expression on Tarvin's face. He also saw the strip of recoprinter paper in his hand. And being who he was he put two and two together.

"Well, now," he said softly, coming forward, treading lightly on the balls of his feet.

The air in Crowther's room was stale and lifeless.

"When you figured out the design for this fortress of yours," Lee commented, wiping his face with a handkerchief, "you forgot to include air-conditioning. I shall be damn'

166

glad when this storm decides to break." He put the handkerchief away. "How long do you intend keeping him here?"

Crowther was still in his shirt-sleeves. There were dark patches beneath his arm-pits and across his back. His massive, pallid forehead was greasy with sweat.

"Only until tomorrow, just long enough for the synthoflesh periphery to complete absorption. The sooner we get him back to his own place the better. The hospital adjustment in the matrix is very precarious. I'm keeping him under heavy sedation while he's here. But even so . . ." His shrug was a ponderous lifting of bulky shoulders. "Have you managed to get a line on his assailant?"

"Not yet. But we will." Lee sounded more confident than he felt.

"The laser-gun?"

"He'll have found a new hiding place for it. This time I've nothing to go on; it could be anywhere in the hills. I'd like to import my own retaliatory lasers but I suppose you would consider that too much of a risk." He glanced sideways, his brows making a question.

Crowther was very definite.

"I would. They're too large for effective concealment. And certainly not capable of p.m. adjustment if Alan did happen to catch sight of one."

"I've put in a request to D.E.S. for a couple of automatics. They'll be better than nothing. I thought I might let Tolley have one, you the other. I've still got the Beretta that was planted by the gate."

"I've never handled an automatic," the other said doubtfully.

Lee grinned. "Point and press. Noisy but effective at short range." He lost his grin. "Incidentally, I've got Verity under lock and key. He had no explanation for how his knife came to be in Alan's possession. The very fact he didn't have a story ready is a point in his favor, but I can't afford to take any chances. D.I.S. is double-checking his records."

He turned as the door opened. Tarvin brought a slip of paper to him. "This has just come through."

Taking the paper Lee queried briefly: "Tolley?"

"Having his breakfast," Tarvin rejoined, and closed the door behind him on his way out.

Lee looked at the message.

"Further report on Gregory Gallea. Age, forty-three. That should narrow the field. Physical description not available." He grimaced. "Never is for External Security types. And apparently he's an agent, grade E. One of the top boys. Same grading as Hagan Arnold was. Yes, here it is: Trained with Hagan Arnold as operational outside contact. Arranged recovery heli-lift. Present at time of crash. That must have been when he got hold of the gun. Traced back to England. And that's all. The usual ending: 'Checking still in process.' "

"Forty-three," Crowther mused pensively.

"Which lets Holt out for a start. His face doesn't owe anything to plastoflesh. He's sixty if he's a day. Tarvin? . . could be."

Then he stopped.

"No need for that. The answer's staring us in the face. Elimination by time factor. Your people — any recent additions? Say within the last six months?"

Crowther saw what he was driving at. He shook his head.

"All regular members of my research staff. Tarvin, three years; Clamp — oh, five at least. Mrs. Low longer than that."

"And only two men have joined my group within the past few months. Holt — and his age lets him out. And Fred Tolley."

Opening the door with one hand Lee slid the automatic from his pocket with the other. Crowther followed him along the passage to the radio room. But only George Tarvin was there.

"Tolley?" Lee barked.

"Not back yet." Tarvin eyed the gun curiously. "But he should have been. He said fifteen minutes. That was half an hour ago."

"Damn!" Lee turned sharply, almost colliding with Crowther. At the door he stopped as a thought struck him, turning back to the room again.

"That message — was it recoduplicated?"

Tarvin bent over the printer. "Yes, the

169

indicator is set at duplicate." He flicked a switch, the printer hummed emptily. "But there's no duplicate here."

Lee slipped the gun back into his pocket with a gesture of bleak resignation.

"So that's it," he said heavily to Crowther. "He returned while Tarvin was bringing me the message, guessed why he was away, checked with the recorder and knew the game was up."

They went back into the passage.

"Five, nearly ten minutes," Lee said, stroking his chin, sizing up the position. "He could be anywhere by now. He'll make for the hills. I'll alert the Blandon Kinery in case he finds the path. But I don't think he'll try to leave the valley. He'll try to finish the job he's started, whatever it is he has in mind. D.E.S. types don't give up easily. Even renegades. At least we know now who one of our invisible enemies is. Verity could be the other. I don't think he is, but I can't release him until I'm certain. That means I'm two men short."

He looked at Crowther. "I need replacements."

"Out of the question," the other rejoined without hesitation. "I can account to the p.m. for the two absentees. But it will be impossible, completely impossible, to adjust it to embrace new personnel. Even you must see that." There was more than a hint of sneer in his voice. And perhaps triumph.

"Then delay his return home long enough

to give me a chance to bring in a squad of D.I.S. security men to comb the valley. Say two more days."

"That neither. I refuse to delay his return to normal conditions by even an hour longer than is necessary. The present matrix addition is extremely precarious and could break down very easily."

"With only two men left," Lee said harshly, "I can no longer be responsible for security."

Crowther wasn't impressed by the ultimatum. He had one of his own to deliver.

"That is your affair. Any attempt to override my authority will be immediately reported to the Prime Director himself."

And with that, allowing no time for a continuation of the argument, he swung on his heel to stalk majestically away, leaving Lee glowering, his face as black as the thunder clouds that coiled about the distant hills beyond the windowless walls of the farm.

Squatting on a slippery slope, his back against a not particularly comfortable outcrop of rock, his hands clasped about his knees, Gregory Gallea stared broodingly at the line of gorse bushes that screened the valley below. He felt that his present position lacked dignity, was invidious, and bordered on the ridiculous. He was also conscious of a certain confusion of mind, an emotion to which, as a trained D.E.S. agent, he was unaccustomed.

171

He had known that sooner or later his identity would come to light. There had been little enough time in which to cover his tracks. Internal Security, grinding slowly and remorselessly like the wheels of God, would trace his movements step by step. But he had underestimated them. Planting Hagan's gun for Hagan to find had been a logical thing to do, but not a clever one. It had given them the link, and as a result he had almost been caught with his pants down.

And but for the inexplicable intervention of George Tarvin, one of Crowther's own pet boys, he would now be tucked away under lock and key, awaiting the coming of night and the helijet that would take him away to be delivered over to the not over-tender mercies of the green-uniformed State Police.

Returning from breakfast — he grimaced — probably the last food he would see for some time — he had seen Tarvin's face and the paper in his hand, and had guessed right away what had happened. But oddly enough there had been no occasion to put into practice his specialized training in unarmed combat. No occasion at all . . .

For: "You'd better take a look at this," Tarvin had said, offering the paper.

He had read the message warily, all the time watchful, assessing the situation. Tarvin was intelligent enough to have realized its import. Yet instead of hot-footing it to Craig, or Crowther, he had shown it to the man to whom it referred. And that hadn't made sense. And neither did the fact he had obviously taken time out to figure out a plan of sorts.

"Hide out in the hills. As soon as it's dark make for Verity's cottage. I'll meet you there. If it's all clear I'll have the back door open. I'll give you five minutes before taking the message to Craig."

And that's how it had been.

Unforeseen. And inexplicable.

Who, what was George Tarvin?

The Tang agent? Could be. The most obvious explanation. But no enemy agent in his right mind would stick his neck out like that.

Gallea was at a loss. He didn't like being at a loss. He glanced up at the sky at another ominous rumble of thunder. Neither did he like the idea of getting soaked to the skin. The storm might hold off but he would have to find shelter of some kind in case it didn't.

Dressed for the part of the family doctor visiting his hospitalized patient, wearing his jacket again, tie carefully knotted, Crowther came breezily into the ward. Karen, for want of something to do — she had found pointless conversation with Alan to be a steadily growing strain — was unnecessarily studying the case cards and temperature charts that had hung at the foot of the bed. She turned with relief at the doctor's entrance. Sitting up in bed, hands clasped behind his neck, Alan watched the scene with a kind of amused tolerance that brought a faint frown to Crowther's forehead.

"And how is the patient, Nurse?" he wanted to know.

Force of old habit made her hand the cards to him. "He seems very well, Doctor."

"He's taken his tablets?"

"As soon as he awoke."

"Excellent." He returned the cards to her after a cursory glance at them. Then he turned his back on the bed while he took a metal case from his pocket and busied himself filling a hypodermic syringe from a plasto-capped vial. When he turned back to the bed he found Alan already rolling up the pajama sleeve of his left arm. Crowther seemed unusually thoughtful while he was administering the injection. When he had finished he slipped the case back into his pocket and rested his hands on the rail at the foot of the bed.

"You will be pleased to hear that you are to be discharged from hospital later on to-day, Alan," he said benignly. "Not that you are entirely well. But the hospital needs the bed." He invited participation in ponderous humor. "If the patient is able to produce a smile then he's fit for discharge. But I will have to insist that you take things very quietly for a few days. Very quietly indeed."

He turned to Karen.

"I have made arrangements with the hospital authorities for you to accompany the patient to his home and stay with him there for a while. He is forbidden visitors until I give the word."

He straightened, ready to leave. "And now a word in your private ear, Nurse," taking her elbow.

And in the passage, the door carefully closed, his voice kept low:

"You're quite certain he took the tablets?"

Karen nodded. "Quite sure."

"There's something —" He broke off, fingering the heavy folds of flesh below his chin. "I had intended moving him during darkness, but I think it might be best to bring the time forward to this afternoon. Immediately he has had lunch I will give him an injection to dull his senses during the journey. I shall use my own car, the blinds drawn. You will be ready at three."

"Very good, Doctor."

Still fingering his chin he turned to look at the door.

"When he came round, did he ask where he was?"

"Yes."

"And how he came to be in hospital?"

She thought back. "Yes, I think he did." But her voice held doubt.

Crowther vented small anger at her. "You know all the circumstances. I thought you would have had enough intelligence to realize that everything he says and does should be carefully noted. You will remember that in future."

He paused to allow time for his instructions to be absorbed. Then:

"I want you to draw him into a conversation about the village. He must be prepared for the absence of two of the inmates. You will tell him that Anthony Verity has been called away to visit a sick relative in Cradhill, and that Fred Tolley has had an accident with his van and will be away for some time. Do you understand?"

Fred Tolley. An accident. Away for some time. . . .

That could mean only one thing. His real identity had been discovered and they had taken him away. She couldn't find her voice. It cost her an effort even to nod.

"That's all for now," Crowther told her.

Stunned, Karen sleep-walked back into the ward. From the bed Alan watched, his expression unreadable.

"And what," he asked pleasantly, "has been happening in Bewdey while I've been in hospital?"

Deep in thought Crowther paced slowly along the passage. He had already observed and noted changes taking place in his patient, the unnatural speed of movement associated with a quickening, an intensification of his reflex actions, the indications that his hearing ability was supernormal, the speed with which his flesh had knit itself to the applied synthoflesh. And now there was something new to be added. For when he had turned his back on the bed while he filled the syringe, he had decided, simply on the spur of

176

the moment and for no particular reason, that instead of giving the injection in the right arm as he had done every time before, this time he would use the left arm. And then he had turned to find Alan already rolling up the sleeve on his left arm. And that could mean only one thing. It was at that point that Doctor Crowther decided upon a revision of his plans.

Instead of returning to his own room he made his way to the one that Lee had appropriated for his own use during his stay in the converted farmhouse. He went in without the formality of knocking. Lee, cigarette in mouth, glanced up with annoyance from the map over which he had been poring.

"A small change in plan," Crowther said almost apologetically. "I have just come from an examination of my patient. He will be fit to be moved early this afternoon. Moving him in daylight will be hazardous from my point of view but should make your task easier. Perhaps you would be good enough to make the necessary dispositions to ensure his safety during the short journey."

"Only too happy to oblige," Lee retorted with heavy sarcasm. "I will use my two men to encircle the valley."

Crowther spread his hands in a conciliatory gesture.

"I appreciate your difficulties. I need Tarvin, but I can place Peter Clamp at your disposal again."

"Thanks." Lee stubbed out his cigarette

savagely. "Thanks for nothing. If you had any concern at all for his safety you'd leave him where he is, where it's comparatively easy to keep easy guard on him. Out there he'll be wide open."

"I have explained already why he has to be moved," said the other patiently. "This place is not part of the p.m. The house is. And once I have him there I can take certain steps to ease your responsibility. He will be confined to his bedroom and I have forbidden visitors. Mrs. Low and Nurse Summer will be in constant attendance —"

"Two women," sneered Lee.

"One is very capable. The other will learn. I also intend to keep Tarvin permanently in the house. With Alan confined to his room his presence will not affect the matrix."

"And just how long do you think you can keep him fastened up?"

"I hope — long enough," Crowther replied, still patiently. "The time needed, as I have impressed upon you before, is something which no one can forecast. I shall have his typewriter taken up to his room and I will tell him that writing will help hasten his convalescence. There is nothing more I can do."

"Yes." Lee looked down at his map. "Under the circumstances — I suppose you can't do more." He sounded mollified.

Crowther said: "I have offered you Peter Clamp. But if you feel you can manage without him I would be grateful. As well as my-

178

self, I would prefer to have two extra men in the house. . . ."

Lee glanced up sharply. "Then take him."

The other inclined his head. "I propose moving Alan at three o'clock."

"Pleasant journey," Lee said.

When the doctor had gone he leaned back, lighting another cigarette and regarding the glowing tip through narrowed eyes. Something, he told himself, was rotten in the State of Denmark. He had the feeling that something was going on behind the scenes. It was only a hunch, certainly, but experience had taught him that his hunches usually paid off. And there were certain facts to support this present one — the way Crowther had played down the seemingly unnatural changes in Alan's behavior, calling them a temporary thing, a phase that would pass once treatment had been adjusted. Had treatment been adjusted? Lee drew thoughtfully on the cigarette. No point in asking Crowther outright, he would only be given an answer that could mean anything.

And now it seemed that the doctor was in an all-fired hurry to get his patient away from the safety of a place that had been converted into what was virtually a fortress, and back in the house where he was to be surrounded exclusively by Crowther's own people. His reasons were logical enough, but then one couldn't expect less from one of the top men of the Department of Counter Psycho-conflict.

179

Lee came to his feet. He felt that the time had come for positive action. Up until now Crowther, using his authority of seniority of rank, had kept him tied hand and foot. That was a state of affairs that couldn't be tolerated any longer. He went into the passage, past the door behind which Verity was confined, and to the radio room beyond. To Tarvin, seated by the main control panel, he said: "I'll take over for the time being. You'd better report to Doctor Crowther. There's been a change in plan."

When he was alone Lee sat down at the bench and spent a few minutes mentally phrasing a message. Then he switched to transmit. His original intention had been to ask for two automatics. Instead he asked for something very different.

12

SOME TWO MILES out of Cheltenham, hidden by a thick screen of trees from the main Gloucester road, was the house that had been requisitioned by the Department of Internal Security to be the outside contact point of Operation Newlife, the relay station, as it were, between Crowther's Bewdey and the Prime Director's London.

Several factors had contributed to its selection. It was fairly close to the artificial village — twenty miles as the crow flies; it was comparatively secluded and inaccessible; it possessed a garage, a rare adjunct in this day and age, that could be converted into a storage place, and nearby was a level patch of land, uncultivated — another rarity — hidden from the casual observer, where the helijet could land and take off on its night trips.

In what had once been the living room, but was now an office, Eric Kitch read the message that had just been brought down from the upstairs radio room. It had come from Lee Craig in Bewdey, and he found it somewhat disturbing. So much so that instead of directing the waiting operator to transmit the usual acknowledgment, he waved him impatiently away while he reread the message carefully, and then spent some time trying to read between the lines.

Kitch, holding down much the same rank as Lee Craig in the D.I.S., was very much aware of his loyalty-inspired responsibility to the State in general, and in this very specialized operation to Julius Minsterly, the Prime Director of that State, in particular. Apart from the acceptance of responsibility he was also the recipient of certain private instructions from the Prime Director, whose apprehensions about the Department of Counter Psycho-Conflict were no secret to his intimates. It had unfortunately been necessary to place a C.P.C. man in charge of Newlife. But it was neither necessary nor desirable that he should be given a free hand. Julius Ministerly, who had ridden to despotic power on the backs of a small band of fanatical followers, trusted no man. In that way only lay survival of the system he had been able to impose upon a country reeling and disorganized from its almost overnight realization of an exploding-population problem, and the immediate harsh rationing of food and clothing to which, as a result, it had had to be subjected.

A Dictatorship was the most powerful form of control. It was also, paradoxically, the most vulnerable, with only one pedestal to be set toppling. That was something he had realized way back in 1966 when he had first assumed the then office of Prime Minister. Five years later he had changed the title to Prime Director of State, and the State Police had come into being.

At the start, the green-uniformed men had worked alongside the blue-uniformed Civilian Police — a relic of the twentieth century — but gradually they had taken over authority until the civilian body had become little more than a token force with no powers.

Both forces came under the authority of the Department of Internal Security, but the State Police constituted what was virtually a private army, equipped with the vicious laser-guns and answerable only to the Prime Director himself. Ostensibly they had been brought into existence to control, amongst other things, maintenance of rationing, compulsory sterilization, and the allocation of child-units, to those State-married couples which had been approved for breeding purposes. They were, in actual fact, the means by which Minsterly kept the population under control.

That State of United Britain was only eleven years old, the subjugation still precarious. No one appreciated the position better than Minsterly. And no one knew better than he that his greatest threat came not from the Sinoasian Peoples' Republic, nor from the people of the new State, but from the insidious clique of psycho-physicists who controlled the Department of Counter Psycho-Conflict. There was a behind-the-scenes struggle that never came out into the open, was unknown of by the population. A cold war between psycho-science and conventional militarism. A chessboard shifting of silent pieces, small power replacing small power. An angling, an inching toward the next step of the ladder. A hidden victory first for one side, then the other. But stalemate, at the moment, with militarism, represented by the followers of Minsterly, holding most of the key positions. A precarious stalemate . . .

Eric Kitch, being who and what he was, was well aware of the situation. He realized too that inevitably the struggle must be reflecting itself between the Psycho and Security factions engaged in Operation Newlife. There had been indications of it in some of the messages that had come through. There was an even stronger one in this latest message.

On his desk was the red scrambler-phone that connected directly with Julius Minsterly's private office. He picked up the phone. Like all D.I.S. men, Eric Kitch was a good servant of the State. He was also a man who never left anything to chance.

The storm held off, but still threatened, purple and thunderous gray behind the hills, barely moving, rumbling ominously. A few spots, isolated thunder spots, spattered the dust, polka-dotting black on brown as Gallea made his way along the path in search of shelter. The rain stopped almost before it had started, and he found a cave of sorts, little more than a weather-scooped recess in

a sloping rocky bank, but by crouching un-
comfortably he would be able to place suffi-
cient coverage overhead to protect him from
the worst if the storm should break. From
the level ground in front he had a fairly good
view of part of the winding road below. He
didn't need his watch to tell him that his
usual time for eating had come and gone. It
was half-past two, he was hungry, and the
morning had been an age in passing.

His eyes caught a stir of movement on the
road. Squatting on his haunches, regretful of
the absence of binoculars, he parted the
ferns to peer out. Two men, their features
too distant to be distinguishable, plodded
stolidly from the direction of the farm. Both
were hatless, both had dark hair. That let
out Cowen and the Major. Both of them were
too stocky for Craig. So they had to be
George Tarvin and Peter Clamp. Both Crowther's men. They disappeared out of sight
and Gallea sat back on his heels.

Clamp could be on his way to his post
office, but Tarvin had passed his shop. Which
meant they weren't on their way to take up
their usual posts against Hagan's return to
his pseudo-home. In any case, according to
Crowther, that transfer wasn't scheduled
to take place till darkness.

Gallea nibbled thoughtfully at a blade of
wiry grass. Craig's prime concern was keeping Hagan safe from harm. That was why
he had collected all the men in the farm. It
was also why he hadn't wasted time and
energy on combing the hills for a one-time

radio operator cum van driver. And yet there were two of his protective force, strolling along like it was Sunday afternoon and they hadn't a care in the world.

And Craig with two men short into the bargain. Gallea found a sense of satisfaction in the knowledge that he was entirely responsible for the two shortages. He had appropriated Verity's knife with one main and one secondary purpose in view. The secondary purpose being to create dissension in the ranks. That had worked fine. But the main purpose, oddly enough, hadn't; Gallea took time out to go over the incident again.

Right at the start of Newlife, during his briefing, Crowther had taken great pains to describe the character of his artificial man. Alan Fraser, he had intimated, was a timid type who presumably wouldn't say boo to a goose and would likely scare into a blue funk at the drop of a hat. That was the picture Gallea had got, but it hadn't turned out that way at all.

Craig's idea of using Alan as bait for a trap was a damned lousy one. The bait, Gallea figured, would stand less than a fifty-fifty chance of coming out of it with a whole skin. It called for a spanner to be tossed in the works. No hope this time of making another phone call, warning Alan not to go to the hills to meet the girl, for anyway, she wouldn't be there. Approaching him directly was completely out of the question. So the only thing to do was wait until he had actually left the house and was on his way, and then scare him into returning whence he came. Hence the dual-purpose purloining of the knife. A timid type, stopped in his tracks by a blade quivering inches from his nose would surely throw what little valor he possessed to the winds and hoof it back home.

But Alan hadn't done that. He hadn't even faltered or changed color. He'd just kept right on going. Which meant that Gallea had had to race hell for leather along the brow of the hill to get to the position Craig had ordered him to take up, before Alan reappeared out of the copse.

Gallea nibbled thoughtfully at the grass. Things had happened so quickly it was difficult to picture them now. He had spotted the stir of movement that gave the ambush away, probably the laser-gun being brought up to shoulder position. The bait was walking smack into the line of fire. That was when things had really got moving. And so far as Alan was concerned, they had moved hellishly fast.

Gallea supposed, thinking back, that he had acted instinctively, sliding down toward the path with the idea of first intercepting Alan and then racing on to try to cut off the assailant's line of retreat. But Alan had reacted so damned fast it had been a plain impossibility. One instance here, the next — a dozen yards away. And then confusion, with the laser churning the path into the flames of hell.

For a creature supposed to be gentle and retiring, as Crowther had made him out to

be, Alan had sure shown unusual talents.
Gallea smiled dryly. So much for one part of
the psycho-matrix. He threw away his grass
and changed his position to prevent cramp.
Then he looked at his watch for something
to do. Reliving the past had used up thirty
minutes. It was just after three. A long,
weary day. Roll on nightfall. He hoped Tarvin would have enough sense to bring some
grub with him when he came to Verity's
cottage. The inhabitants of the artificial
village lived virtually from hand to mouth,
drawing their supplies daily from Tarvin's
shop. There would be no cache of biscuits
and cheese in Verity's larder.

A car moved slowly — crawling, almost —
along the road. Gallea leaned forward to
watch it, reading and understanding the
message of Crowther's black sedan, all the
blinds drawn. So there had been a change in
plan. Alan was being moved in broad daylight. No point in guessing wildly at the
reasons behind the changed schedule. He
wondered if Karen was tucked away behind
the drawn blinds. Most likely she was —
playing her part as a nurse. He wondered if
she knew what had happened to Fred Tolley.
Was there any need for them to have told
her? There was. She would have to produce
some kind of answer when Alan, back into
his home routine again, got round to asking
questions about absent friends.

And then he wondered, oddly enough —
because Gregory Gallea rarely took time out
to ponder about the opposite sex, and when

he did, he generally thought about them only in derogatory terms — whether she fancied herself to be in love with Alan Fraser. Certainly, she had only met him a couple of times, but a lot can happen during a few hours' interchange of confidences in the seclusion of a sunny hillside.

It was bad, very bad, if she did feel that way. He hoped fervently that her feelings for Alan were no more than those of sympathy and the desire to be of help. It was inevitable, either way, that she would get hurt. It would be inconceivably worse for her if she were in love with a man who had no real existence. He wasn't worried about Alan on the same score. Crowther had been very clear upon one point. Sex hadn't been included in the psycho-matrix.

Karen was attractive. . . . Gallea judiciously selected another stalk of grass. And intelligent. Look at the way she had figured out for herself that he was for Alan, and then had the nerve to tell him so in front of Craig himself. She had guts as well as intelligence and looks. . . .

And according to Cowen, the State had investigated and approved her heritage, had checked her health and passed her as suitable for Approved Marital Union and subsequent breeding. A healthy animal, fit to perpetuate the race. Gallea bit through the stalk. Romance under a June moon . . . That was out. Julius Minsterly, in his wisdom, didn't approve of such haphazard methods. So silvery moons, dancing twilight seas, and the frag-

rance of June roses were all out. Good blood
stock was the deciding factor these days. This
is the woman I have selected, says the man.
Check, comes back the State in due course.
Okay, you're both group six, child-unit allocation, one. Here is your permit, signed and
sealed by the Department of Mental Hygiene,
subsection Marital Unions. Take it along to
the local padre. Just for the show. The bless-
ing of the church. And the church itself
licensed to hold congregations, the padre licensed to preach. So long as every sermon is
first submitted for State Censorship. So
much for young love under the high-riding
moon. Gallea threw the grass away with a
savage gesture.

Nearly an hour had passed and there was
no sign of Crowther's car returning. Which
probably meant it had been tucked away in
the trees, in the place they had had to use
for vehicles ever since Alan had wised up to
a van that hadn't returned, and a car that
had pointed to instead of away from the
mythical township of Cradhill. Which
further meant Alan had been dumped back
home, all set to take up the reins of his artificial existence again.

Gallea sized up the sky again. Clouds were
still building up. The air was thick enough
to cut with a knife. Normally it would start
to get dusk about half past nine. But it
would go dark early tonight, by the look of
it. It would take him about an hour to work
his way round the valley toward the back of
Verity's cottage.

At eight o'clock he left the cave and the ledge where he had spent most of the day. An hour later he was crouching amongst the bushes a stone's throw from the cottage. The clouds had almost met overhead and rain was spitting again. Dusk came quickly, the drawing of a curtain. Soaked to the skin now, for the rain was coming down heavily, he saw a flicker of light in one of the cottage windows. Minutes later the back door was opened. Lightning forked viciously, the cottage was a cardboard cut-out in a world filled with blue-white light, and thunder came crashing and rolling, echoing back from the hills as he raced, head down, toward the sanctuary of the open door and the kitchen.

A small torch had been propped on the table, its shaded beam directed away from the door. Tarvin stood waiting behind it, his dark face shadowed and saturnine in the half-light.

"A night for ducks," he said, and thunder crashed out again.

And in the silence that followed, broken by the steady drumming of rain, with Gallea mopping his streaming face with a futile, already soaked handkerchief, another voice spoke from the shadows.

"Gregory Gallea, I presume," said Crowther with a certain lack of originality, advancing into the light, rubbing his hands and beaming genially.

The handkerchief still to his face, Gallea

froze, recovered from his surprise and shrugged resignation.

"A distinguished reception committee," he observed evenly.

They were still in the kitchen.

"We have a great deal to discuss," Crowther had said. "We can't talk in the dark. This will be the safest room. We've already checked for dublems."

Tarvin drew the curtain across the tiny window, closed the door against the rain and switched on the light. He had brought food, a small packet of bread and sliced meat. "The best I could manage. I'm afraid you'll have to wash it down with water." Then he brought a small electric fire from one of the other rooms, plugged it in and helped Gallea strip off his sodden outer clothes. Feeling slightly ridiculous in vest and underpants Gallea sat on the table while his discarded clothing steamed over the back of a chair.

He took the unnatural meeting with Crowther in his stride. It was obvious that he hadn't walked into a trap. There was an oddly friendly atmosphere about the place. Tarvin was helpful, Crowther smiled, and the food was good. And outside, by the sound of it, the heavens had opened.

"You must forgive me for talking while you are eating," Crowther said. "I can afford very little time. First things first. You were obviously responsible for the telephone calls and the planting of the gun. I am also fairly certain that you were responsible for Verity's knife finding its way into Alan's possession."

Gallea swallowed, broke off a chunk of bread and was sparing with words.

"I used it to try to scare him back into the house."

"I thought it had to be something like that. From what I know of you, you intended no harm to Alan. On the contrary. You have been trying in your own way to protect him. Our feelings are mutual. The idea of using him as bait for a trap was none of my doing. I did my best to prevent it. At that particular time Craig attached more importance to trapping the enemy agent than to protecting Alan. He regarded it as a calculated risk. Do you understand the position?"

The curtained window became a momentary oblong of blazing blue light. Thunder crashed and echoed. Then the drumming of rain.

"No," Gallea said. "I don't understand the position."

"No." Crowther drew up another chair and sat down, resting his elbows on the table. "Gregory Gallea, born in London in nineteen seventy-three. Drafting from school to State Police Cadet Force. Transferred to training establishment of Internal Security. Later transferred to D.E.S. Trained with Hagan Arnold as dual overseas agents. In 2009 was posted to —"

"You've made your point," Gallea broke

in. "All right. So you've got me tabbed. So what?"

"So I know you were Arnold's friend although you never actually met. So I know you think much the same as he did."

"I'll grant you that," Gallea said, and motioned toward the sink. Tarvin, leaning against the wall, unfolded his arms, found a cup, filled it at the tap and brought it to the table. Another cannonade of thunder seemed to rock the cottage.

"I haven't made a point of studying your records," Crowther said. "The information I collected about you was only incidental. My man was Hagan Arnold."

"Your man," Gallea echoed over the rim of the cup.

"You're not making it easy for me. I need your help. To get it, I'm prepared to lay all my cards on the table."

"My help?" Gallea set the cup down. "All your cards?"

"Face upward." The other leaned forward intently. "I'm going to tell you what I am doing to Hagan Arnold, and why."

"I'd already figured that out."

There was a tense silence. Crowther glanced quickly toward Tarvin and then back to the table again.

"And just what am I doing with him?"

Gallea bit on a slice of chicken.

"You're out to give him a new personality and background. You're hoping he will accept it without question."

The other inclined his head. "Obviously. And the reason?"

"Not to get him to cough up that information. That's just an excuse. You figure that if you can get away with it with Hagan, you can do the same to anyone else. Then you'll go in for mass-production. Slaves of the State, all set out in rows like dolls in a twentieth-century shop window. All neatly tagged."

Tarvin gave vent to a sharp bark of laughter.

"You disappoint me." Crowther shook his head. "I had expected better of you. You couldn't be further from the truth. What I am attempting to do is entirely the reverse."

Gallea stopped chewing. "The reverse?"

"You were correct in assuming that I was using the urgency of obtaining the information from Hagan Arnold as the excuse for Operation Newlife. I was, in fact, able to obtain the information from his subconscious while he was still undergoing plasto-surgery. My department has already taken the necessary steps to counter the most unlikely threat of our television transmitters being employed by infiltrated enemy agents as a weapon of video-induced mass-hypnosis. The Tangs are ingenious, but inclined to be over-imaginative."

He paused to assemble words.

"You will be familiar with the general situation in the country. Julius Minsterly assumed power eleven years ago. Since then the population has existed under the burden of a ruthless, military dictatorship, a burden intolerable to free-minded men. There is only one organization strong enough to afford resistance. My own department, that of Counter Psycho-Conflict.

"It is controlled by psycho-physicists, intelligent men who have the welfare of the country at heart. Where the possibility of overthrowing the present régime is concerned, white coats and hypodermics are useless against green uniforms and laser-guns. The revolution, when it comes, will be bloodless. But first we need a figurehead, someone to offer in place of Julius Minsterly. We need someone with great intelligence and with great personal courage. A giant amongst men. Homo Superiorus. Nietzsche's Overman. We have such a man in view."

Gallea drained his cup and carefully set it upside down on the table. The paper which had been wrapped round the food he screwed into a tight ball and balanced it on top of the inverted cup.

"Hagan Arnold," he told it.

Crowther leaned back.

"He was first brought to our attention some eight years ago. He seemed to have the potential of what we were seeking, and so we took him under our wing. Without, of course, his knowledge. He made no secret of his opinions. But for our unobtrusive interventions he would almost certainly have been forced to undergo Correction. He found the dictatorship utterly detestable. He expressed certain ideas to an alternative form

196

of government. To help those ideas coalesce we arranged for him to attend a course of Comparative History of the Second Elizabethans at a university. Our intention, once he had completed the course and had been thoroughly indoctrinated in the governmental methods employed during the latter part of the twentieth century, was to have him transferred to a Psycho Establishment of our choosing for further study.

"Minsterly could have had no idea of what we had in mind. It was only by chance that he arranged for Arnold to be drafted for duty behind the Bamboo Curtain within weeks of his leaving the university. At that point we had to consider him a write-off. As you are well aware, it is rare that an agent sent behind the Curtain is able to return."

"Hagan," Gallea said softly, "was the first."

Crowther raised his brows. "I hadn't realized the fatality-rate incidence was so high. Arnold was indeed fortunate. . . ."

Thunder crashed suddenly, followed by a prolonged distant rumbling. The rain had ceased to drum.

"That's one way of looking at it," Gallea said coldly as the peals died away.

"You are thinking about his accident. Certainly, he was very badly burned, but not, as is now apparent, irreparably so. We were able to give him a new face."

"And a new mind."

"Let me try to explain, in simple terms,

197

what has happened to him. The accident triggered off the psycho-block, reducing him to a state of complete amnesia. As soon as we received news of the accident I arranged for a team of my physicists to jet out to inspect him. They decided his condition was malleable. It was at that point that I personally contacted the Prime Director and obtained his full authority to use any means at my disposal to obtain from Arnold's mind the vital information. The authority was granted with the one, and anticipated, proviso, that Internal Security must also take part in the operation. Otherwise, I was to be in charge, given a comparatively free hand.

"I arranged for Arnold to be jetted back to England. During the process of giving him a new face I managed to obtain the information. But that knowledge I confined to myself and a few of my associates, Professor Tarvin here included. Once the synthoflesh grafting was complete I had Arnold moved to my own laboratory."

Crowther paused reflectively.

"I have tried to make clear the motives that activated my associates and myself. Our ultimate aim was the deposition of Julius Minsterly. What I did to Hagan Arnold was solely for the good of the country."

"All very commendable," Gallea observed dryly. "And just what did you do to him?"

"I cannot go into the details of the technique involved, a combination of surgery, mechanico-deep-hypnosis and treatment with drugs. We all possess certain parts of

198

the brain which normally remain dormant. What I did was to activate those parts of Arnold's brain. It was a complete reversal of the Correction process. Instead of deducting, I added. Bringing him here, to this very specialized environment, was the final stage of the treatment.

"Although his memory had gone he still retained certain basic instincts, one of which was his yearning to live in the past of fifty years ago. This yearning we had already fostered, solidifying it, when we had arranged for his period of intensive study. He now accepts, without question, because his subconscious wants to accept, that he is living in the year 1966.

"Because of his exhaustive knowledge of that period we have had to take great pains to ensure that every detail of his life here is correct down to the smallest detail. It is essential he finds not the slightest flaw. He is certainly happier now than at any other time in his life. It must be granted to few men to have such an impossible dream fulfilled."

The window was outlined in a fierce blue blaze. The electric light flickered. Thunder came crashing out. Tarvin padded across the room to lift one corner of the curtain while he peered out.

"You still haven't told me what you have done to him," Gallea said. "So you probed about inside his brain. What would that do?"

Crowther spread his large white hands on the table and stared down at them. It seemed that he was reluctant to be pinned down to a hard and fast explanation.

"I am sure we are agreed that the country must have a change of régime," he said carefully. "In Hagan Arnold's mind are all the details of the form of democratic government proven effective in the past to cope with extensive restrictions without having recourse to force. That is the type of government we need to replace the present military dictatorship. To head it, to replace Minsterly as Prime Director, we need a man with exceptional talents."

"You've already made that point."

"My probing into Arnold's brain, as you describe it, was designed to furnish him with such talents. I think I may say I have been successful. Because of the presence of Internal Security personnel it has been necessary to keep him under heavy sedation to prevent his rapidly developing faculties from being remarked upon before we are ready to put them to use. Even so, certain of them have become manifest, to the extent of drawing attention and comment. I cannot be certain that the explanations I offered were accepted."

Gallea said: "I figured there was something odd about him. I didn't know whether I was imagining it. . . . Just before he got lasered he seemed to move like greased lightning."

"The result of a speeding of his reflex actions, purely involuntarily. He would not, at least at that time, be aware of anything unusual. Neither will he be aware of his increased rate of metabolism. The syntho-flesh graft applied to his laser burn would in a normal person take at least four days to become established. In Arnold it took less than two hours. Which gives rise to certain interesting possibilities. A wound which in someone else might prove fatal, to him would seem little more than a scratch, healing almost immediately. The same resistance will almost certainly apply to infection, perhaps even to the normal degeneration of bodily tissue, relating in a prolongation of his life span."

Gallea's leathery features settled into an unreadable mask.

"And tampering with his brain did all that?"

"And many other things. It is, very simply, a question of mind over matter. The brain controls the workings of the body. When previously dormant parts of the brain become activated, that control becomes intensified. Normal functions will increase in value. Vision, hearing, taste, smell, will all become more acute. There will be the appearance of completely new senses; precognition —"

"Precognition?"

"Merely a forward extension of the reflexes. Literally, the ability to be able to see into the immediate future."

Crowther paused.

"You must understand that what is happening to him is in no way supernatural.

The power of precognition, one facet of extrasensory perception, is inherent in each of us, but undeveloped simply because it is related to part of the brain not normally used. From time to time there are instances of such senses manifesting themselves naturally, without surgical intervention. This leads to the inevitable conclusion that one day mankind will learn how to make use of such powers. The possibilities are boundless. Telekinesis, teleportation . . ." He lifted his hands. "Even, perhaps, immortality."

"And Hagan is all this?" Gallea asked in a tight voice.

"That is what he will ultimately become. How long it will take before the process is complete there is no way of telling. We are dealing with a piece of machinery that has become rusty with neglect and disuse."

"You said you needed my help."

"Your clothes are dry enough," Tarvin said, swinging the chair away from the fire. "You can make yourself respectable again."

Gallea stood up to slide his legs into still-steaming trousers.

"Well?" he asked Crowther, steadying himself with one hand on the table.

"You could compare Arnold to a child who has just discovered the art of walking, instinctively wants to show off but hasn't learned control. If no help is forthcoming it could do itself harm. I need your help in controlling Arnold."

Gallea fastened his belt. "I got the impression you were doing fine with sedatives."

"Up to a point, yes. I had been giving him what I considered to be the minimum effective dosage. After his new reflexes became evident I increased the dosage. But apparently not sufficiently. Another sense has shown itself. Telepathy. He now has the ability to read thoughts. Left to his own devices he may try to leave the house."

Gallea tucked in his shirt. It was clammy and uncomfortable.

"There is no reason why he should," he grunted.

The other hesitated at that, glancing sideways at Tarvin, giving the impression that here was something that had been previously discussed.

"Arnold has new powers at his disposal," he said, turning back to Gallea. "He must be aware of them by now. We have to go on established facts. Sudden power can induce a feeling of superiority."

"Megalomania," Tarvin said bluntly, in the tone of one who has no desire to waste time in mincing words.

Gallea struggled into his jacket.

"You are afraid of him getting out of hand."

"Not in the way you mean," Crowther told him. "I'm not afraid of what he might do, but what would be done to him if he fell into the hands of Internal Security. Arnold, still not yet able to control his new senses, unwittingly gave away his telepathic ability to me. He would do the same to Craig. And Craig, already suspicious, is no fool. He would guess what was happening and take steps to prevent it. And apart from the threat of discovery we still have to cope with the enemy agent who has already had two attempts to kill him and will undoubtedly try again."

"You have problems," Gallea said.

"I have taken all available measures to counteract them. Clamp, Mrs. Low, and Nurse Summer are in the house with him now. He will not be left unguarded at any time. There is one other thing that must be done. It is for that I need your help."

"The storm seems to be passing over," Tarvin reported from the window. "It's almost stopped raining." He blinked at a flash of lightning. "I spoke too soon."

"He must be given another injection," Crowther said. "One that will put him under total sedation. If I were to approach him he would read my mind and resist. I am someone he hasn't yet learned to trust. You are different. His instinct will label you as a friend. He would be prepared to accept your intervention, knowing from your mind that you intend him no harm. The only other alternative is brute force, something I abhor and which could have disastrous results."

"You are asking me to give him a shot of dope?"

Tarvin, prowling impatiently about the room, collected two raincoats from the sideboard, handed one to Crowther and draped the other loosely across his shoulders.

"A simple hypodermic injection," Crowther said, coming to his feet. "Well?"

Gallea rang the inverted cup with his fingernail. "Thanks for the food," he told Tarvin. He looked at Crowther. "I don't suppose I have any choice. If I do refuse you can't very well let me go in case I decide to risk my neck and take the story to Craig."

"I am not relying upon threats to ensure your cooperation, but upon your affection for Hagan Arnold," the other said blandly.

"Yes." Gallea adjusted his tie. Even that was damp. "Let's get it over with."

Tarvin switched off the light and used his shaded torch to find the way along the narrow passage. He went ahead to open the front door and peer carefully about, satisfying himself by what little gray light remained that the road was empty, both the adjoining cottages in darkness.

He walked some distance in front, head bent, shoulders hunched against the rain-mist and the night.

"A very able physicist," Crowther remarked conversationally, drawing his coat about him as he walked. "Responsible amongst other things for a new technique in diathermic-thalamic incisions."

"Spare me the small talk," growled Gallea.

When he reached the last corner before the houses Tarvin waited while they came abreast. All three walked on in silence. Another few minutes brought the two houses into sight, gloomy shapes against the stormy sky, brought into sudden ghostly life by a pale flash of lightning. The windows of the first were blank rectangles. The front door of Alan's house stood wide open, yellow light spilling across the sodden drive.

With an exclamation Tarvin leaped ahead, Gallea close at his heels, the older man following some distance behind. A crumpled shape on the hall floor was Mrs. Low. Tarvin dropped to his knees at her side.

"She's alive." He looked up the stairs. "Craig?"

Gallea took the stairs three at a time, filled with a cold fury born of his concern not so much for Hagan Arnold's safety as for Karen's.

A door stood open. Karen lay across the threshold, her face turned upward, her eyes closed. Beyond her the room was empty, the clothes on the narrow bed piled in disorder.

13

THE STORM still hung over the valley, lightning dancing along the hills, thunder rumbling almost unceasingly. In his shirtsleeves, his massive face lined and gray and greasy with perspiration, Crowther straightened wearily from the bed where Karen lay still unconscious.

"Well?" Gallea asked harshly from the window.

"No physical injury apart from intensive bruising down one side, presumably where she hit the door." Crowther laid a syringe aside. "She's suffering mainly from shock. I've given her something. She should be coming out of it soon."

The door opened and Tarvin, also jacket- and tieless, came to stand at the other side of the bed.

"Shock," Crowther said briefly to the unspoken question on the dark face. "Mrs. Low?"

"She came round. Now she's sleeping. Something had caught her an almighty smack across the back of her neck. She didn't see who or what was responsible, but she doesn't think it was Craig or any of his men. She and Clamp were in the kitchen, they heard a noise, and she came to investigate, thinking it was someone trying the front door. She saw a movement out of the corner of her eye and that was all."

"What about Clamp?" Gallea put in.

Tarvin shook his head. "No sign of him."

Gallea looked at his watch. It was quarter past ten.

"When did all this happen?"

"She thinks it happened about fifteen minutes or so after we'd left to meet you. Which makes it the best part of an hour ago."

Gallea turned to the window. He could see nothing but his own face staring back at him, distorted by the rain-flooded glass into an unrecognizable leering mask. Hagan was somewhere out there. He felt certain that he hadn't gone of his own free will. Someone had struck Mrs. Low a vicious blow and flung Karen ruthlessly aside. Hagan was incapable of both those things.

He spoke on the impulse of the moment.

"I think it might be a good idea to take the risk of a trip as far as the farm."

"Don't be a fool," Crowther said in a dispassionate, almost disinterested voice.

Tarvin qualified equably: "No point in doing anything until the girl comes round and we hear what she has to say."

Lightning blazed out, thunder rolled, ending in a crashing crescendo of sound. The lights flickered and died. Tarvin's voice came from the blanketing darkness, swearing in a level of monotone. His torch flashed.

"Probably a power pylon struck by lightning," Crowther remarked unperturbed. He was fumbling in his case. The beam of a second torch came to join the first. He propped it on the chair so that its light bathed the bed.

Gallea turned back to the window. With little light behind, his reflection had faded and he could make out the dark shapes of trees. It seemed to him that there was a faint brightening of the sky behind the hills. Certainly, the rain seemed to be easing.

Crowther's voice exclaiming soft satisfaction brought him round to face the room again. Karen had opened her eyes and was making an attempt to push herself upright. Gallea went quickly to the bed, thrusting Crowther's bulk unceremoniously aside.

The dazed look in Karen's eyes gave way to recognition. He slid a supporting, protective arm about her shoulders. "It's all right, Karen." He followed the direction of her eyes. "The storm's put paid to the lights. They'll soon be on again." He leaned closer. "Can you tell us what happened?"

Her gaze moved away, discovered Crowther, moved to Tarvin's darkly impassive features, returned to rest on Gallea's anxious face. Her eyes, he saw, seemed to be guarded and wary rather than fearful. And yet the pupils were dilated and he sensed by the tenseness of her shoulders that she was fighting hard to retain self-control.

"He went away," she told him almost inaudibly. "Alan. He just got up and went away."

Crowther's voice was filled with urgency. "You must tell us everything that happened."

"I was sitting"— she turned her head to look toward the window —"over there. I must have dozed off. Only for a few minutes, I think. When I woke up he was sitting on the side of the bed. Then he just got up and walked out of the room."

"You tried to stop him," Crowther hazarded.

She avoided his direct gaze. "He didn't see me. He pushed me to one side. It was an accident."

"No," Crowther said roughly, pushing Gallea aside and stooping over the bed. "You fainted from shock. There's more to it than that. It is essential for his own sake that you tell us everything that took place."

She looked over the solid shoulders toward Gallea.

He nodded reassuringly. "I was wrong before. They're not using him as a guinea pig. At least not in the way I figured. You'd better do as he says."

"He was — different." She closed her eyes.

"Appearance?" demanded Crowther impatiently. "Behavior?"

"His face had changed. It was still Alan's, but like a caricature. Swollen . . . bloated, like a puffy rubber mask. It was —" She raised a trembling head to her forehead. "His eyes and mouth seemed pushed to-

210

gether. . . . Smaller, like a baby's. His hair —" She broke off again. "He sat on the side of the bed and smiled; not at me — at nothing. I don't think he even noticed me. When I tried to stop him leaving he just put out his hand and pushed me away."

Crowther straightened slowly, looking at Tarvin.

"Accelerated metabolic progression."

"Superprogressive," Tarvin said judiciously. "First, development of previously dormant faculties, then compensating adjustment of containing vehicle. A logical sequence. If we could determine the point at which control failed, we —"

"Forget the lecture!" Gallea broke in roughly. "Where is he likely to have gone to?"

Tarvin shrugged. "Julius knows."

"By now," explained Crowther in the tone of one using single-syllable words to an imbecile, "his mind will be something completely alien. It will not be using the same reasoning processes as ours. It will set its own standards based upon a feeling of contemptuous superiority, and so his actions will be unpredictable. He will certainly be reveling in his newly discovered powers. His behavior gives some indication. . . . Hindrances in his path were brushed disdainfully aside as beneath his notice, as we would flick away the annoyance of a fly."

"His new powers?" Karen breathed.

He ignored her, moving away toward the

door, joined by Tarvin, both mouthing technicalities that were meaningless to Gallea.

"They had the bright idea of trying to improve upon nature," he told Karen when they were alone. "Amongst other things he can now turn his hand to mindreading." He spoke lightly, deliberately, minimizing the situation, not wishing to make things worse for her than was necessary.

She closed her eyes and leaned back without replying. Gallea watched her for a few moments before returning to the window, fretting at his enforced inaction. It had stopped raining and the horizon sky glittered with returning stars. He could see the gray band of the road.

He had read between the lines of the lecture Crowther had tried to put across. All right — so they wanted a bloodless revolution. He could go along with that. And the fact they needed someone to step into Julius Minsterly's shoes. But they intended keeping that someone's unusual talents under control, under their scientific thumbs, drugged, using him as a puppet figurehead, only bringing him out into the open from time to time, relaxing the sedation enough to scare the pants off the populace whenever those pants needed scaring off. Like a freak in a circus sideshow. A weapon of authority. Minsterly used his green-uniformed boys. The Psycho crowd intended using Hagan Arnold. A change from a military to a scientific dictatorship. Back where you started, only worse. Out of the frying pan into the fire.

But they had bitten off rather more than they could chew. Their tame superman had got out of hand. Progression, Tarvin had said; adjustment of containing vehicle . . . logical sequence . . . He knew what that meant. Hagan's body was changing to balance his new powers. Instead of making themselves a man from the past to rule the present, they had got a man from the future on their hands. A kind of ironic justice.

A shadow moved on the road and Gallea stepped instinctively to one side of the window. It had been making toward the house. He glanced at the bed. Karen seemed to be sleeping. Picking up one of the torches he opened the door. A soft murmur of voices had to be Crowther and Tarvin, presumably mulling over their problems in the privacy of one of the darkened rooms. He cupped his hands over the torch, allowing just enough light to filter between his fingers to show him the way down the stairs, along the passage to the kitchen. Switching off the torch he opened the back door to slip noiselessly into the still-dripping garden. His eyes, already dark-adapted, picked out the outline of the lawn and the screen of bushes beyond. The shape — a man's shape — had been making toward the side of the house, possibly with the intention of entering by the back door. Gallea went swiftly, ghost-silently, across the grass, turning when he reached the bushes to crouch, waiting.

His body tingled ice-pleasureably. Now he was in his natural element. This was what he had been trained to do, pit his wits and cunning against another. Now he was indeed Gregory Gallea, one-time agent of External Security, and not Fred Tolley, deliveryman. His mind automatically evaluated the situation. He had the advantage. He was aware of the intruder's presence.

Not Hagan. He had the feeling that Hagan, able to read thoughts, would now know about everything that was happening. His mind, so Crowther had said, would be reveling in its new powers. In Craig and his security personnel he would see a hindrance. Hindrances were to be thrust ruthlessly aside. . . . Gallea fancied that right now Hagan was probably somewhere close to the farm.

It could be Peter Clamp returning, but if so, why the obviously stealthy approach? One of Craig's men doing a reccy? That was a possibility, but a most unlikely one. If Craig was suspicious enough to want to know what was happening in the house, then vested in authority, he would come openly. That left only the enemy agent. But the boys wouldn't come unarmed, and a laser-shadow had been empty-handed. The Tang gun was too damned bulky to be concealed about the person.

Gallea, crouching away from the revealing skyline, eyes narrowed, frowned. Logical reasoning had failed to come up with the intruder's identity. Which wasn't so good. He liked to be able to anticipate. His frown relaxed into a fleeting grin. He could use a dash of Hagan's precognition talent right now.

The seconds ticked by. Still nothing moved. His ears caught a rustle of sound that could have been anything. If the shadow had been making for the rear of the house it should have come into sight some time ago. As he came cautiously upright his nose caught a faint smell of burning. So far as he could tell it seemed to come from the direction of the bushes and trees that divided the two houses. He retraced his steps slowly across the lawn, this time keeping well inside the shadow of the hedge. The smell grew stronger, resolving itself into smouldering wood and cloth, and something else. Something that turned his blood to ice and made him quicken his pace.

He stumbled over the body without seeing it. One quick flash of his shielded torch revealed the hideous charring, the smoke still rising from burned foliage, from the ground, from burned clothing and seared flesh. Peter Clamp's face had miraculously escaped. He was still alive, but with those smoking wounds, had to be dying. Gallea crouched, not able to use his torch or even his voice for fear of revealing his presence to whoever had used a laser-gun not a few moments before.

Clamp had recognized him in the brief torch flash. His lips moved. Gallea bent his head to catch the few whispered words.

"Followed — lost him — moved too fast

215

— someone else — coming toward house — tried to —"

Clamp's eyes glazed, his mouth fell open. Gallea straightened slowly, his mind working automatically, encompassing new factors, fitting them into a picture.

This was the first time an attack had been directed at anyone other than Hagan. Which was significant. . . . A change of policy. Something must have happened behind the scenes to make it imperative for the Tang agent to dispose of Hagan now, without anymore time being wasted on undercover subterfuges, even at the risk of discovery.

Gallea knew a great deal about the yellow men. He knew how their minds worked. First aim, achieve success at any price. If they could do that and live to operate another day, so much the better. If not — then out into the open, get the job done and to hell with the consequences. The old creed of kamikazi. Kill, and be killed, but take as many of the enemy with you as possible. And that looked like being the position right now.

All right. So much for the new background. The Tang must obviously think that Hagan was still in the house. Would he go in after him? Too damned right he would. Complete with laser, all set to burn down anyone who happens to cross his path. Like Peter Clamp . . . It would be some time before he would be able to free his nose of the smell of charred flesh.

Gallea made his silent way back toward

the lawn. Karen was in the house, and the knowledge was an icy emptiness in his stomach. Urgency screamed soundlessly in his mind, telling him to go racing heedlessly inside, shouting a warning. Cold reason told him that he would get himself lasered for his trouble and with nothing achieved.

He stopped when he reached the corner of the house, flattening himself against the wall, listening. The steady dripping of rain-heavy branches had stopped. Everywhere was still and silent. The slightest sound would carry quite a distance. The sky had almost cleared and the world away from the darkness of the trees was filled with pale starlight. Once he turned the corner he would be out of the shadows and fully exposed. And the Tang could be anywhere — behind him, waiting in the bushes ahead, even already inside the house. Gallea didn't look forward to the prospect of crossing the exposed length of wall to the back door.

He dropped to a crouching position, preparatory to making a dash for it, and by so doing saved his life. The blue-white beam came lancing across the lawn, turning the wall above his head into a hissing, crackling circle of disintegrating brick. He rolled sideways into the bushes, and the beam followed, churning into the ground and then flicking out of existence. Gallea inched backward under the bushes and then lay still, pressed tightly to the ground, hardly daring to breathe. He guessed that the attack had been temporarily lifted because the Tang, not in a position to obtain replacements, would want to conserve the power-pack of his weapon, using it only on clear targets.

He raised his head cautiously. Through the matted branches he could see the expanse of lawn. A man had emerged from the shadows and was coming across the grass, half-stooping, the laser-gun held at waist level, its muzzle moving in short sweeps, ready to lance death the moment anything moved.

And Gallea moved, collecting himself for another sideways roll, and a branch snapped. The Tang stopped, the weapon pointing directly at Gallea's hiding place. Tensed, he waited for the inevitable. Instead, inexplicably, the bull-shouldered man suddenly stopped in his tracks, staggering as if struck by an invisible assailant, the muzzle of the gun dipping, then the weapon itself sliding heedlessly from his grasp to the ground.

Gallea rolled clear of the bushes and came crouching to his feet, watchful and alert, filled with mingled relief and puzzlement. The other, hands clasped to his face, was rocking on his feet, lurching backward and forward in the grotesque travesty of a dance. As Gallea went toward him he dropped to his knees and then toppled face downwards on the sodden turf. Gallea snatched up the gun, holding it ready while he stared in disbelief at the now motionless figure. He touched it tentatively with his foot then stooped to grasp the bulky shoulder, turning it so that the face pointed upward. The features had been twisted and distorted almost beyond recognition by some inward fury. And he was obviously dead.

Holding the weapon slantwise across his chest Gallea made his way thoughtfully back to the house. The lights came on as he reached the hall. Crowther and Tarvin, brought from one of the bedrooms by the sound of his footsteps, stopped at the sight of the gun.

"Craig is another man short," Gallea said laconically. "And so, I'm afraid, are you." He held up the laser-gun. "With this, Peter Clamp."

"Who — ?" Tarvin started, but Crowther was there first, speaking evenly, almost conversationally.

"I'm sorry about Clamp. He was a very able scientist." He lifted a large white hand in a vague gesture of dismissal. "So you managed to dispose of the second invisible enemy. That should please Craig." He smiled without humor. "Now, I always had certain suspicions about our village constable."

For all Gallea wasn't feeling very proud of himself he still found some pleasure in his small moment of revelation.

"You put your shirt on the wrong horse. Now we know why the gallant Major Holt liked to enjoy a fire every evening. He wasn't so much playing the part of a soldier who had spent blood-thinning years in the tropics, most likely he was born in the Far East. Behind the Bamboo Curtain."

He paused.

"And you were wrong again. I didn't dispose of him. Something else did that for me. Otherwise I would have gone the same way as Clamp. The body's on the lawn. I think you ought to take a look at it."

They used one of the downstairs front rooms as a makeshift mortuary. Leaving Crowther and Tarvin with Holt's body Gallea went upstairs, taking the laser-gun with him, having no intention of letting it out of his sight. Karen was sitting placidly on the side of the bed, hands folded in her lap, a trained servant of the State waiting for her next instructions. He propped the gun against the bed, seated himself at her side and told her briefly what had happened.

She reached for his hand. "Poor Mr. Clamp . . ." She regarded him intently. "What do you think killed the Major, Gregory?"

He had an answer, such as it was, to that.

"I think I have a coincidence to thank for my being here. Remember his red face? Choleric. Blood pressure. Or did you never get to see him?"

She nodded. "Once."

"Heart attack. He was no chicken. Not the best type for an agent. I suppose they chose him — the Tangs — because he looked so typically English. Or what they think typical."

But a heart attack wasn't the answer. He had seen death in many forms too often. But never with a face so distorted as had been Holt's. Something else had killed him. Something inside, twisting relentlessly, agonizingly. He had never seen death come that way before. Shifting, his foot touched the butt of the gun and he found an odd reassurance in the contact. And pleasure from the touch of Karen's hand that still rested on his.

Footsteps were heavy and measured on the stairs, tread by solid tread. Crowther came to stand in the doorway, silent for a few minutes, fingering his thick upper lip, gazing from beneath heavy brows, his gray face unfathomable.

"I would like a few words with you, Gallea," he said finally. His eyes moved to Karen. "In private would be best."

Gallea came to his feet, Crowther stepped aside to let him pass, then closed the door behind him, nodding back toward the room.

"I assume you are able to use that?"

"What?" Gallea was first puzzled then startled. "The laser. Yes, I've handled them before. Not that I was keen on the idea. You're not thinking in terms of Craig?"

"Not Craig." Crowther's tone was ponderously significant.

Gallea fumbled for his cigarettes without taking his eyes from the other's face.

"Without a complete post-mortem," Crowther said, "it is impossible to tell what killed Holt. But we are able to make an extremely accurate assessment. There are certain indications. . . . And we knew what to look for. We know who must be responsible. It's too late now even to consider attempting to control him. He's learned how to kill. What he's done once he will do again."

"You're only guessing that Hagan was responsible."

"We're certain, and so it becomes necessary that he be destroyed."

"Just like that." Gallea took a cigarette from the packet. "And you've picked me for the job." He was suddenly quite furious, only containing himself with an effort. "You've got a damned nerve!"

"I had expected that to be your reaction. I know how you must feel about him. He wasn't only your coagent, he was also your friend. But there's something you don't know. The man out there isn't Hagan Arnold."

"He was before you gave him a new mind."

"No." The other shook his head. "It's not like that at all. I've got to make you understand. Arnold died on the table while we were operating on him. He was dead for six days. Then we reactivated the body."

He broke off with a gesture of hopelessness.

"There are many things we can't be certain about. Conventional religion tries to find answers for some of them. The thing that gives life to a collection of bones and tissues, is it a soul? Or is it a series of electrical impulses? Or is it something else?"

"I thought you people had answers for everything," Gallea heard himself saying harshly.

"We try to find them. We think that what the church calls the soul, we know as the subconscious. That isn't a new idea. The theory was first put forward as long ago as the start of the last century.

"Hagan Arnold died. That is a solid fact. We infused new life into his body by reactivating the impulses. But the thing that left it when he died didn't return. We proved that by exhaustive tests. The man we call Alan Fraser does not possess a subconscious in the sense of the word. Instead he has a store of instincts and memories. It would take too long to explain the difference."

"How do I know you're not giving me a load of rubbish just to get me to do your dirty work?"

"Don't take my word alone. Talk to Tarvin. He was there. And Mrs. Low. They'll both tell you the same. If you want it in its simplest terms, then Hagan Arnold is dead, and the thing called Alan Fraser is made up of someone else's repaired body, an inheritance of vague instincts and an artificial past. And a brain that had been stirred into new activity.

"It was human — as we understand the word — only as long as we were able to keep its mind under control. You know what has happened. The mind developed faster, becoming more powerful, than we had anticipated. Amongst other things it has complete control over the metabolism of the containing bodily envelope. It is changing that container to something more compatible with its new powers. What the ultimate will be there is no way of telling. We gave it the brain of man as he will be in the far distant future. It is now in the process of giving itself a matching body. Can you understand that?"

"One thing I do understand," Gallea said; "if you are correct in saying he killed Holt, then he also saved my life."

"You have the inheritance of Arnold's instincts to thank for that. His mind probably picked up two conflicting series of thoughts, one friendly, asking for help, the other alien and threatening. He reacted accordingly. That is all. It won't be very long before the inherited store of instincts becomes submerged by the newly developing personality. That is why we cannot afford to wait any longer. Apart from anything else, you are the only one who would stand a chance of even getting safely within laser range of him."

"Laser range . . ." Gallea took the still unlighted cigarette from his mouth, crushing it slowly between his fingers while he thought, letting the shreds fall to the carpet. "If all you say is right, I'll only be able to have the one stab. If that. Certainly no second chances. Which means nothing must be left to luck. Close range, say a hundred yards, no more. It won't be pleasant. But he's got to be found first. It'll be like looking for a needle in a haystack."

"No," Crowther told him. "He won't make any attempt to hide. He will be supremely confident in himself, contemptuous of everybody and everything. He has nothing to fear from anyone."

Gallea spread his hands palms upward and stared down at them.

"Hagan Arnold," he told them in disbelief, and then looked up into Crowther's waiting eyes. "I can't do it."

"When you find him you will feel differently. He never looked like Hagan Arnold. By now he won't look like Alan Fraser. You will be destroying something so alien that it might have come from another planet."

There was no escape from the inevitable. Gallea knew that this time Crowther had told him the truth. Everything pointed to that. It was, after all, Karen who had actually seen and described the start of the change. Crowther was doing the only thing possible in having him destroyed. And there was only the one man capable of tackling that job. . . .

Gallea drew a deep breath of resignation.

"All right. But it will be useless to start searching now, in darkness."

Crowther looked at his watch.

"At first light then. You'd better get some sleep."

But with the coming of first light came something else. The misty, pearl-gray morning was suddenly filled with a sullen, insistent throbbing that brought them all —

Gallea with the gun ready under his arm
— out through the front door to stand in a
small dismayed group staring up the valley
to where the dawning sky behind the farm
was filled with rapidly enlarging glistening
specks.

Thirteen helijets they counted, beautiful
and evil, twelve painted the dark green of
the State Police, and the other, larger, silvery, and sleek, unmistakable to anyone who
had seen it before.

And Crowther had seen it before.

"I had been wondering," Gallea said, eyes
narrowed, watching the formations of three
as they circled above the farm, "what had
suddenly stirred Holt into furious activity.
He must have known the green boys were
coming."

Crowther said in a dead voice: "And Julius Minsterly has come with them."

14

FILLING THE MISTY MORNING with the evil, ear-jarring thrum of throttled-back engines, the helijets maneuvered, metal birds of prey, changing formation with a slick, well-drilled precision, forming a circle above the farm with the Prime Director's silver, multirotored monster in the middle. As one dropped away, sinking to disappear behind the trees, so the remainder adjusted positions, closing the gap in the protective circle.

"A conference in the offing," Gallea interpreted wisely. "And they're not risking ground to air communication. But then the green boys never take chances. Especially with the great Julius himself watching operations. The day of reckoning is at hand. Craig's patience finally became exhausted. Very soon now this valley won't be a very healthy place for yours truly."

He glanced sideways at Crowther who stood apart from the little group made up of Karen, Mrs. Low, and Tarvin.

"You should be all right if you keep your head. Come up with the right answers and you'll have nothing to worry about." He added dryly: "Apart from the failure of your takeover bid."

The bottom had dropped out of Crowther's world and his face made no attempt to disguise the fact. Apprehension bordering upon fear had reduced his features to a quivering, putty-colored mass. The hand he raised aimlessly to his face was shaking. It was the first time Gallea had seen his ponderous self-composure shattered. He found a morbid pleasure in witnessing authority having a bad moment, an experience generally reserved for the little people. But there was no time to be wasted in thinking in terms of poetic justice. He inspected the sky with an expert eye.

"It should take about an hour for the sun to rise enough to clear the ground mist from the hills. I've had dealings with the airmobile green boys before. They believe in keeping their heads in the air and their feet well off the ground. They'll come scouring at treetop level, and they'll wait for the mist to clear first. They've got everything buttoned up and all the time in the world. In any case, they haven't come to look for me. I'm just a side issue. They're obviously here because Craig started smelling a very nasty smell. Which I don't blame him for. I'd have done exactly the same."

He smiled at Karen. "I think you'd better give me directions to find that secret path of yours."

"Where will you go?" she asked worriedly.

"Once I'm away from here I can soon lose

myself." He spoke with more confidence than he was feeling. "That sort of thing's right up my street. It won't be the first time. I've got friends in the right places. A new identity and I'll be able to laugh at even the great Julius himself."

Karen left the others to come quickly to his side.

"I can show you the way myself, Gregory."

He raised startled eyebrows. "Yes. I suppose you could, at that." Then: "There's no need for you to take to the wild open spaces. They won't do anything to you. You're not in their bad books."

"I'd rather come with you," she persisted.

Gallea turned thoughtfully to regard the others. Mrs. Low had moved back into the doorway and was standing placidly enough, hands folded in front of her, her face expressionless. Tarvin was at Crowther's side, and Crowther himself was obviously making an effort to pull himself together. Equally obviously he still had a long way to go.

"Got your alibi all worked out?" Gallea asked him. "All the details cut and dried? Great on details, the green boys. You could start off by putting them in a good mood. The operation has finally proved successful and you've managed to winkle the information out of Alan's subconscious. That should make Minsterly happy.

"The winkling took place last night, and it required a certain amount of persuasion. Alan got all steamed up as a result, panicked, and made a run for it. Or something along those lines. Season it with a dash or two of scientific gibberish and you'll get away with it.

"Holt died a natural death, just after he'd disposed of Clamp. And if they don't like the coincidence, they'll just have to grin and bear it because they won't be able to prove he didn't die naturally. The laser-gun — you can just say it wasn't there. They'll assume that I probably whipped it, which can't be helped. You were all set to start searching for Alan when the helis showed up and you decided to let them do the donkey work for you."

"They mustn't find him," Crowther said with an effort.

"It might be tricky," Gallea admitted. "but you can rise to the occasion. The change in his appearance is accidental, a sort of by-product of the treatment you have been subjecting him to. Even scientists make mistakes sometimes. Minsterly will like that."

Crowther brooded silently and unhappily.

Tarvin urged: "There's nothing else you can do."

Gallea showed his teeth. "Not unless he's keen on having a dose of his own Correction medicine."

Talking, he had been moving away from them, one watching eye on the hovering circle, the other on the steadily rising sun. He had reached the corner of the house and Karen had followed.

He smiled at her. "Our tame little nurse.

That uniform suits you. You should wear skirts more often."

He lowered his voice.

"I don't go along with Crowther and his schemes, but he represents the only opposition in the country to Minsterly. If anything were to happen to him — and Minsterly only wants an excuse — then what little organized resistance there is would fold up. That's why I tried to help him out of a spot by providing him with a cover story. I think he'll make use of it. If you were to come with me it would leave a gap in the story."

"He could tell them I ran away to try to find Alan."

"No, lass." He shook his head. "They'll find Alan, but they won't find you. Or me. They'll put two and two together and come up with collusion. You helped me escape. Crowther allowed one of the staff to fraternize with a traitor. They won't like that."

It was the only excuse — partially true for all that — he could offer for not taking her with him. She was only safe so long as she remained at the house.

Karen wasn't prepared to give up so easily.

"It's impossible to try to describe the path. I'd have to show you the way. You'd never find it by yourself."

He threw another quick glance in the direction of the farm. The halo of glistening metal was still there, but the helijet that had earlier dropped out of sight had now reappeared, soaring up to join the others.

He spoke sharply, roughly.

"I tried to let you down lightly. There's no time now for politeness. I don't want you to come with me. I don't want a woman clinging to my coattails."

The harshness achieved its purpose. She was stunned, as he had hoped, into acceptance of the situation.

"Go along the hill path until you come to the fork. Then you have to turn to the left and climb to the clearing where I met Alan. The path starts from there. It's easy to follow at first, but after a while it —"

The thrumming changed into a pulsating roar that gradually increased in volume.

Stooping, only a little—for he wasn't much taller than she — he kissed her on the mouth and then was away without a backward glance, through the trees and bushes between the two houses—there was the charred place where Clamp had died — following the hedge alongside the lawn, into more bushes, through them with practiced agility, through the hedge and out into the misty open. Running, head low, he reached the cover of the copse as the first helijets came roaring overhead.

Six of them were immediately above the house, dropping until they were almost at roof level, until he could see through the plasto-windows the shadowy shapes of the men they carried. Five hovered — where were the others? and Minsterly's silver opulence? — and one went plunging out of sight toward the front of the house.

And that one, Gallea told himself, would certainly be the same one that had landed at the farm. Only now Craig would be on board. He could picture his face, smug, self-satisfied, triumphant in the authority of having Julius Minsterly himself at his elbow. All set for the showdown to end all showdowns. Looking forward to seeing Crowther rubbing his nose in the dust. But if Crowther could remember his lines everything should be all right. They would thrash the thing out, and then they would start scouring the hills for the artificial man. And at the same time they would be keeping a sharp lookout for a renegade one-time radio operator. A dual mopping-up operation. The green boys had a rooted objection to loose ends.

Holding the gun across his chest Gallea made his way through the miniature glade, not hurrying, taking it easy, walking almost jauntily. At the other end of the copse he took time out to check the power-pack of his weapon. He estimated that there was about one minute's firing time left. He smiled more with wry resignation than grim humor. You can do a whole lot of damage with sixty seconds of laser beam used in short bursts. And a helijet presented a fairly hefty target. But the men inside would be armed with lasers of their own and with the advantage of being behind heat-resistant plasto and tribo-tensile steel plating. A gorse bush would be worse than useless against a beam that could smash through a brick wall. All things considered his only policy would be to cast valor to the winds and keep his nose to the ground, only moving when the coast seemed clear, prolonging the thing for as long as possible in the creed of while there's life there's hope, only using the gun as something to go out with in a kamikazi blaze of glory.

He assessed the outlook. The mists were already beginning to lift. His first port of call would be a fairly large clump of bracken perhaps a hundred yards up the slope. He peered upward and backward through the branches. The thrumming echoed inside his head but the helijets were out of sight behind the trees. As he turned he caught a flicker of movement from the corners of his eyes and he swung on his heel, bringing the gun to waist level, its muzzle covering the glade. Karen came running toward him and he lowered the gun as she flung herself into his arms. One arm about her shoulders he watched the glade behind. There was no sign of pursuit.

"What brought this on?" he demanded roughly.

Her voice was muffled against his chest.

"It landed on the road. . . . Policemen climbed out. . . . They all had guns. . . . Mr. Craig was with them and he was in uniform too."

"So you threw a panic." He pushed her gently away, holding her at arm's length. Her hair was in disarray, one black tendril falling over her forehead, and she had lost the scrap of linen that had served as a hat. Her passage through the bushes and hedge had ripped the upper part of apron and left scratches down her bare arms.

"I was frightened," she said simply.

"Did anyone try to stop you?"

"Only Mr. Tarvin. He tried to grab my arm."

He regarded her closely. "There's something else, Karen."

She shook her head dumbly.

"You've had dealings with the green boys before," Gallea said. "And you're far too sensible to be scared by uniforms and laser-guns. So what happened?"

"I just want to come with you." She slipped urgently from his arm. "We mustn't stand talking. We must go before they come after us."

"We're not going anywhere," he told her. "There's no place to go."

Her pupils dilated at the cold certainty of his voice.

"You were going to try to find the path —"

"They'll have men waiting at the other end. There's no way out of the valley. That's why I wanted you to stay behind. You'd have been safe with Crowther. The only reason I left was because I'm supposed to be hiding out in the hills and Crowther wouldn't have been able to explain my presence away." He gripped her shoulder, trying to impart his own urgency. "You've got to go back now, before it's too late. Tell them you panicked. They'll understand. They're used to that sort of thing."

"No," she said obstinately.

He sighed resignedly.

"I can't take you back. That would connect you with me. Which leaves only the one alternative." Letting the gun fall he drew back his clenched fist. "I'm sorry about this, Karen. . . ."

"It's Alan!" she blurted, and he lowered his arm. "Alan?"

"He's frightened. I heard him, just before the helijet landed."

He stared at her. "What do you mean, you heard him? Was he there?"

"No," she shook her head. "I heard him once before, just after they'd brought me here. I thought it was a dream until I heard him again." She raised one hand to the side of her head. "In here . . . I wanted to try to find him before —"

"You mean you can read his thoughts?" he asked incredulously.

"I don't know, Gregory. It's hard to explain. The first time it was just like something talking inside my head, for me, for my benefit. This time it was more like overhearing someone without his knowing."

Relaxing his grip he stooped to recover the gun.

"You were afraid I might find him and try to use this on him."

"I don't know what I thought"— miserably —"I just turned and ran."

236

He said slowly: "Crowther wanted me to kill him. I think he'd almost persuaded me it was the only thing. But I didn't intend looking for him. If I had come across him it would all have depended upon —" He stopped.

"How much he'd changed?" she supplied wisely.

"I suppose so. Crowther says he isn't Hagan Arnold at all. Nor Alan Fraser. He says he's nothing. But I can't believe that." He stared at the gun. "I don't know what to believe. Nothing makes sense." He glanced up again. "Can you hear him now?"

She shook her head. "It only came for a few seconds."

"And you're quite sure you haven't been letting your imagination run away with you?"

She shook her curls in vehement, indignant denial.

"All right," He grinned fleetingly. "But it doesn't change things. I still want you to go back. And if it makes you feel any easier I promise that if I do happen to stumble across him, which is most unlikely, I won't try to harm him."

She was indignant again. "That wasn't why I came after you. I was frightened. And I knew you'd never be able to find the path by yourself. They may not be watching the other end like you think. It comes out in a wood and it's only people who've lived in these parts who would know where to look."

"The green boys aren't people," Gallea

said dryly. "They're experts. It's a thousand to one chance they won't have been able to find it."

"But there is a chance," she urged.

"Yes," he admitted, still hesitating. "I did have the stupid idea of making a heroic last stand. If you tag along that's out, which is just as well. So when they do find me I'll surrender peaceably and tell them you were trying to find Alan, found me instead, and I had some idea of using you as a hostage." He rubbed his chin ruefully. "Which stinks. I'll need time to think it over. For the time being I'll have to play it as it comes."

He stepped backward and looked through the branches. What he could see of the sky was still clear.

"All right, Karen, I'll give you best." He turned, pointing. "We make for that biggish clump of ferns. If there is a ghost of a chance then we'll have a stab at it. Let's go."

They left the shadow of the trees to climb the slope. Mist still pooled the hollows but the sun had breasted the hills and was flooding the valley with the bright promise of a fine day. Karen, a few paces behind him, slipped on the sodden turf, exclaiming aloud so that he stopped and went back to help her. They were breathless by the time they reached the bracken. Behind it was an exposed patch of sandy soil that had almost dried out, and he dropped to his knees, pulling her down with him, then leaning forward, parting the fronds to look out.

Above the house the five helijets still hovered. Between the trees he could just make out the tips of two of the rotor blades of the one that had landed. And the others? He lifted himself. With Minsterly's silver craft they were still a circle over the farm. He looked at his watch and was surprised to find — for so much seemed to have happened since first light — that it was only a few minutes past eight.

He looked back over his shoulder. Another slope and then the path, bordered by gorse bushes that might screen them from the village but not from the air. Karen's white apron would stand out like a signal beacon. He touched it. "You'd better take that off. I should have thought of that before." When she had untied it he rolled it into a bundle and thrust it deep into the bracken. "How far to this clearing of yours?"

"I've never been this way before," she said frankly. "I can't remember if Alan mentioned how long it took him. But once we reach the fork it's only a few minutes' climb to the clearing."

He came to his feet. Karen went first this time, he followed, ready to steady her should she stumble. It took five minutes to reach the path. Now they could see the helijet that had landed on the road. A row of green beetles — seven, he counted — stood by the tripod undercarriage. What he could see of the drive was empty. Apparently the thrashing-out process was being conducted indoors. That would be Craig's idea. A background frieze of blank-faced, uniformed men, a table upon which he could rest inquisitorial elbows, a chair that would accommodate his uniformed rump while Crowther stood on the metaphorical carpet in front. A tribunal all to himself. "When did you last see your patient?" Gallea grinned sardonically at the evoked picture.

"The coast's as clear as it will ever be," he said to Karen. "Keep your head down, make the most of what cover there is and if we're spotted get as far away from me as possible." And when her brows queried: "They may shoot first and ask questions afterward. It's me they're gunning for. No point in our both getting"— he was going to use the service word "crisped" but thought better of it, substituting —"into trouble."

The steady droning of distant rotors was a monotonous, menacing accompaniment. Walking along the path he felt naked and exposed, but the slopes above and below offered no more cover than they already had, and the uneven ground would only retard progress.

He fancied that from this distance they should be undetectable to the naked eye, but if any of the green boys happened to have binoculars trained in their direction then they could call it a day.

The path swung to follow the contours of the slopes. The road and the cottages came into view. Gallea felt some relaxing of tension. But ahead now was a massive spur that carried the path on its unclothed weathered shoulder, thrusting it out into the valley with no cover of any kind so that negotiating it they would be fully exposed. They rounded the spur with their backs toward the steep upper slope. At the other side, with the fork now in sight, Karen released her pent breath in a quivering sigh of relief that became a startled, involuntary exclamation, bringing Gallea to a halt, his eyes raking first the sky then the valley.

But she hadn't seen anything. One hand to the side of her head she seemed to be listening.

He guessed then what she had heard. "Alan?" and she nodded, still listening intently.

"It's gone again." She let her hand fall. "I heard him just for a few seconds. But very clearly. I don't think he can be very far away. He knows we're here and that we're in danger. I think he was trying to warn me of something."

Gallea's eyes rested on the fork ahead and then lifted to assess the slopes. She interpreted the direction of his gaze.

"The clearing, Gregory . . . is that where he is?"

"We shall soon find out," he said.

But they had been seen rounding the spur. One of the helijets above the house broke formation and was racing across the valley before Gallea, studying the slopes, was aware of what was happening. The sudden roar swung him round on his heels, and then his instincts took over, one hand clamping on Karen's shoulder, thrusting her ruthlessly to the ground. Then he was sprinting toward the fork to hurl himself behind a clump of heather. Rotors churning, jets screaming shrilly, the helijet came roaring toward them, banking steeply as it swung to follow the spur. His face sideways on the ground he watched the shadow swoop monstrously across the slopes while the roar reached an ear-splitting crescendo. The din lessened and he lifted his head cautiously.

The helijet was poised in front of him, low over the valley, almost on a level with his eyes, close enough for him to see where one of the plasto-windows had been slid aside to allow the muzzle of a laser-gun to protrude. He threw a quick glance in Karen's direction. She was still too close to him for her safety. Coming to his feet, crouching low, he turned to plunge upward, forcing his way through the matted undergrowth, heedless of raking briar and gorse, each instant expecting the world to burst into sudden, searing flame.

But he reached the clearing safely, dropping to his knees the moment level ground was beneath his feet, finding cover of a sort behind a small outcrop of rock. Chest heaving, the breath tearing at his throat he watched the hovering, motionless helijet, saw how the laser muzzle had traversed to cover his new position.

And others were coming to join it. Two were raking across the valley from the direction of the house. Those above the farm had changed formation and were sliding toward him, two lines of three with the huge silver craft between. Still breathless from the fury of his climb Gallea turned to look at the clearing.

And at first sight it seemed to be empty, a small level place perhaps a score of yards across, bounded on one side by an arc, a miniature amphitheatre of tumbled stone, at the far side by dense undergrowth with more rocks thrusting through the branches, one a tall smooth mound about the height of his waist, a chalk, for it was almost white, looking like a gigantic mushroom — and on the third side by a low screen of gorse and briar. Gallea turned to look back at the valley.

Overhead, immediately overhead so that he had to strain backward to watch them, the silver craft and its escort seemed to fill the sky. In front of him the first helijet hovered watchfully. And a little way along the slopes one of the others was coming in low, its tripod extending like the claws of some monstrous bird of prey, its undercarriage almost touching the bushes. As he watched, one of the doors opened and a metallic ladder came snaking out, a man already swinging to set foot on the swaying rungs.

And then, as at a signal, the long-expected beam came lancing from the helijet in front,

243

not aimed at him but at the slope below, blasting a fiery circle in the undergrowth, flicking out of existence to leave in its wake a cloud of billowing, acrid smoke.

And that was finally that. It was a marvel they had waited so long. Shrugging bleak resignation, Gallea came to his feet to toss his gun aside and raise his hands in a token gesture of surrender. He turned to regard the clearing, wondering absently if it would be wide enough for the craft to land on.

And the white mound of rock moved.

It swayed gently, as if rocked by a breeze, and at first he thought that the smoke had blurred his vision. But as he moved toward it, stooping, he suddenly realized with a cold chill of horror that drove everything else from his mind that he had found Hagan Arnold.

There were the limbs at the base, almost hidden by the grass, thin, spidery arms and legs, shriveled, shrunken almost out of existence, matching the hideous mockery of features, the eyes, ears, nose, and mouth that were little more than indentations in the yellow-white, blue-veined parchment flesh. A being — a thing that was a brain and little else. A brain that had no need to see, to hear, to eat. Progression. They had said. Into the future. And was this ultimate man?

Fear, wild, unreasoning fear came pounding into his mind, sweeping away even the horror, swinging him round, sending him stumbling blindly away toward the edge of the clearing. He was only dimly aware through the waves of terror of people moving along the path below. Craig was there, and Karen, State policemen, weapons held across their breasts, and Crowther and Tarvin. Fear drove him on, swinging him round again, away from the slopes. As he stumbled along blue-white fire lanced in front of him, turning the ground ahead into an impassable holocaust.

Another avenue of escape blocked he stopped, turning automatically to look at the helijet that had fired the warning shot. He saw the sudden wavering of the rotor blades, saw them slow and come to a quivering stop, the craft swinging out of control then plummeting downward to strike the ground with a rending crash.

For a brief moment of time nothing happened. Then twin lasers lanced from one of the escorting craft. Gallea flung himself desperately away from the clearing, rolling down the slope, crashing through the bushes until brought up against a rock ledge with a body-shaking jar. He was lying face upward, staring at the curved silver belly of Minsterly's helijet, almost knowing what was going to happen, seeing the same sudden wavering of first one and then all of its eight rotors, watching the nose tip clumsily, all grace gone, the craft slipping sideways, swiveling out of the sky, hurtling down into the clearing with a deafening, ear-splitting concussion. Debris fountained upward and outward from an exploding engine. Metal hurtled toward him and he ducked instinctively as it went thrashing through the undergrowth. He saw another piece coming but was too late to avoid it. Agony burst from the side of his head and blackness came driving from nowhere, carrying him along with it.

When he came round he was lying on the verge of the clearing. A rough hand under his armpit jerked him to his feet. On each side of him were green-uniformed State policemen. More of them clustered about the piled wreckage. Crowther was with them, apparently in command of the situation, issuing orders for the raising of part of a rotor assembly. And Craig was there, hatless, standing away from the others, hands on hips, the sunlight glinting on his shoulder insignia. Seeing Gallea on his feet he came striding toward him to demand "You all right?"

Gallea was startled at the solicitude, brusque though it was.

"Yes, sir."

"Did you find him?"

There was only the one "him" he could mean. Gallea nodded toward the wreckage. "Under that lot," he replied laconically, and then waited for the inevitable orders for them to take him away. But instead the other merely nodded and turned away to go back to his original position.

There was an air of ordered, efficient haste about the tangled wreckage. A blue dancing flame was a laser slicing through metal. Gallea discovered Karen standing at the far side of the clearing, and was surprised again when no restraining hand was laid on his shoulder when he started to move toward her.

She greeted him with an attempt to smile.

"That's the girl." He put his arm about her waist. "Quite a spot of excitement one way and another."

She nodded, her eyes searching his face, her hand reaching up to touch the side of his forehead, the light touch making him wince. His own fingers found a raised patch of bruising.

"I'll live," he told her lightly, and turned to watch the toiling men.

"Was he here?" she whispered.

He nodded. "I'm afraid so. He wouldn't have stood a chance." He kept his face turned away from her. "He'd changed a little. You know — you saw for yourself. This is the best thing that could have happened."

She followed the direction of his gaze. "And the Prime Director?"

"Nothing could have lived through that," he said, and tried to envisage, but failed because of its magnitude, what was likely to happen now.

A jagged section of metal fell clear. Crowther straightened, glanced about him, saw

Gallea, and left his work to come quickly
toward him, grasping his arms and drawing
him to one side.

He spoke in a low, even voice.

"You're in the clear. I told Craig that you
guessed some time ago what was happening, that you saw it as a possible threat to
the State and tried to stop it. I told him
that you came to me to give yourself up
shortly after Alan had divulged the information and escaped, and that then you volunteered to search for him and destroy him.
Craig accepted the story."

"I'm obliged," Gallea said dryly. "So I'll
live to fight another day as well." He
stressed the last two words.

"I thought you had that in mind." A faint
smile touched Crowther's thick lips for a
fleeting moment. "And did you find him?"

"He's under that lot," Gallea said for the
third time, and the other nodded without
any surprise.

"I fancied he would be. He was responsible
for all this. I don't suppose the body will
even be recognizable." He sounded disappointed.

"So what happens now?"

"We don't know yet that Minsterly is
dead," the other replied smoothly, and Gallea looked closely at the bland, unreadable
face before turning, frowning, to watch the
ordered bustle about the wreckage. The
first body was being brought out. When
Crowther hastened toward it he went with

248

him. He watched eighteen more uniformed bodies brought out and laid in a row on the grass. He was there when careful hands lifted out the broken body of the Prime Director to set it reverently down for Crowther's inspection.

On his knees, Crowther finally looked up. His gaze found Gallea's face first and moved quickly away from it, encompassing the waiting, anxious circle of men whose main purpose in life was to protect Julius Minsterly and whose existences depended upon the régime he represented.

"He's still alive," he told them.

They had taken Minsterly to the farm. They had improvised a stretcher, laid him on it and carried him to the pulley suspended from a hovering helijet. Now the bodies of the dead policemen were being hoisted to other helijets, one at a time, a slow, laborious job.

Before leaving to accompany his patient Crowther had spared time to personally inspect the wreckage. There had been nothing else to bring out. Whatever had been underneath had been crushed out of all recognition.

Gallea and Karen made their way toward the road, not returning by the path by which they had come, but going now in the direction of the farm. They had received orders from Craig. They were still both members of Internal Security. There was work waiting for both of them.

Gallea had much to think about. He had seen death come in so many different ways that he felt sure of his ability to recognize it when he saw it. And it had been there in Minsterly's gray, angular face with its high, polished cheekbones, in his staring eyes and wide, bruise-purpled forehead, in his blood-matted silver-white hair and small, pointed beard, in his broken, sagging body. But Crowther had said he was still alive. And Crowther, of all people, would rather see him dead. There was something here that didn't make sense.

They walked in silence.

Karen was also aware of something that didn't make sense. She tried to persuade herself that she had imagined the voice that had spoken in her mind back there in the clearing, Alan's voice, coming to her along after the crash, while they were still searching for the bodies, clear and unmistakable, telling her as it had once before, not to worry, that everything was all right.

15

He opened his eyes.

White emptiness drifted, hardened, solidified, became a ceiling. A light glared harshly. He closed his eyes against the brilliance, reopening them when he had moved his head sideways. White blankness again, but this time a wall. The room took shape as he moved his eyes. A door, a metal and glass trolley, a white-enameled cupboard, a gleaming sink in one corner, another wall, windowless like the first.

His body felt stiff but he was able to move arms and legs. He was lying in a bed and someone was standing at his side. His eyes found a new focus. A woman, young, dark hair, a blue and white dress, a face that was familiar. . . . There was a name for her but it refused to take shape.

She was smiling at him, reaching to touch a bell-push, asking:

"And how do you feel, sir?"

She had called him "sir." He was accustomed to being treated with deference and respect. He was someone in authority and his name was . . .

His fingers reached up to explore the con-

tours of his face, discovering the bony aquil-
inity of a nose, hollowed cheeks, jutting
brows, moving wonderingly downward to
find the even greater unfamiliarity of mus-
tache and beard.

"Mirror," he said, but there wasn't one in
the room.

"When the doctor's seen you, sir," she told
him.

The doctor. His memory supplied a name,
Dr. Crowther, and a face to go with it, before
the door opened and the doctor came to stand
at the foot of the bed, rubbing large hands,
smiling, greeting him, calling him "Mr. Minsterly. . . ."

His name was Julius Minsterly, and he
was the Prime Director of State.

But that wasn't his name, and the face he
had touched hadn't been his face.

The nurse — the uniform, for all it was
old-fashioned, told him that — he would remember her name soon — had one arm
round his shoulders and was helping him
up into a sitting position. The doctor was
filling a hypodermic syringe from a rubber-
capped vial, and the nurse was rolling up
the sleeve of his pajamas. There was the
sting of the needle, the icy touch of spirit
soaked wool, the doctor's voice saying jovi-
ally: "And that's pincushioning over for this
morning. . . ."

And he was someone else, in another place
at another time. A room that was familiar,
sunlight streaming through the window, a
desk, a typewriter, piles of papers. . . .

252

"He asked for a mirror, Doctor," the nurse said.

Nurse Summer. Miss Summer. Karen . . . Three blue bows on a white blouse, golden-brown corduroys, a clearing on the hillside . . .

"Then we must get the orderly to find one for him," said Dr. Crowther, and went to open the door, calling: "Tolley?"

Tolley. A rickety green van laboring along a lane. Fred Tolley, and another familiar face to fit another familiar name, even before its owner appeared to confirm the mental picture.

"Do you think you can find a mirror for Mr. Minsterly, Tolley?"

A smiling nod, a few minutes waiting, then an oblong of polished steel was set in his hands.

"Will that one do, sir?" Tolley, still smiling. "It's a shaving mirror."

He laid it on the bedclothes, covering it with his hands, white, vein-ridged hands that belonged to a stranger.

"Can I be alone?" he asked them.

The doctor was hesitant. "You have been very ill, Mr. Minsterly. . . ."

So he raised his voice, ordering imperiously: "Leave me."

They went away, closing the door behind them, leaving him alone.

He held up the polished steel. A narrow face, high, sloping forehead, a wealth of silver hair, a pointed beard. A face he had never seen before.

And then he was back again in that other room, standing now at the window, watching the reflection in the tree-shadowed glass, seeing another face, solid and ordinary, scar marks at the temples, red-brown hair thick and crisp. The features melted, changing form and color, the hair black as night, teeth gleaming whitely against bronzed skin.

There was no need to search his memory for names. They came of their own accord, filling his mind with pictures, with events, with knowledge and understanding.

He lay back against the pillows and sent the tentacle of his mind out into emptiness, searching for other thoughts.

He found those of Professor Amos Crowther of the Department of Counter Psycho-Conflict who had once brought a dead man back to life, and now had done the same again, and with still the same purpose in view, to create a mockery of a man, a subservient being, a puppet to dance to the bidding of invisible strings, ready to reassume office as Prime Director once the treatment was complete.

He found the thoughts of Lee Craig, high-ranking officer of Internal Security, relieved that Julius Minsterly was still alive, rejoicing in the knowledge that things would go on unchanged.

He found those of Gregory Gallea, one-time agent of External Security, one-time friend of Hagan Arnold, mourning now his death, but at the same time relieved at the dying of the thing that had once been Hagan Arnold.

He reached finally into the mind of Karen Summer and found there a conclusion of thoughts and emotions. Some were sharp and clear, others too entangled one with another for him to separate and identify. There was clear sorrow for the death of Alan Fraser; pity for that man while he had still been alive; fear of the change she had seen in him; relief in his death because of that change; remorse because of that relief. There was anxiety and puzzlement — and this was something she was trying to thrust out of her thoughts — because she had heard, or fancied she heard, his voice talking to her after he had died.

The man on the bed smiled to himself, closed his eyes and looked into the future.

He was an artificial creation called Alan Fraser.

He was a man who had died and come back to life called Hagan Arnold.

He was neither of these, but a little of each and something — a very great something — more.

He was a superior being, far above these groveling, mindless creatures who surrounded him with their senseless thoughts and petty emotions.

And he was the Prime Director of State with the country in the hollow of his hand. And not only the country, but the world.